I0531082

MRS. HENSWORTHY'S BOOKCASE^2
INTERDIMENSIONAL COMMERCE

*Another Tale of Science Fiction, Served with
Tea and Biscuits*

By

Norman J Barta

BALINOR BOOKS
2024

Copyright © 2024 by Norman J Barta and
Balinor Books

Fair Lawn, New Jersey
BalinorBooks@gmail.com

This book is a work of fiction. Any references to historical events, real
people or real places are used fictitiously. Other names, characters,
places, and events are products of the author's imagination, and any
resemblance to actual events or places or persons, living or deceased,
is entirely coincidental.

All Rights Reserved

Except for use in a review, no part of this document may be
reproduced or transmitted in any form or by any means, electronic,
mechanical, photocopying, recording, or otherwise, without prior
written permission of the publisher.

Manufactured in the United States of America

ISBN Number: 979-8-9891371-7-6 (Hardback)
ISBN Number: 979-8-9891371-8-3 (Paperback)
Also available as an eBook

Library of Congress Control Number: 2024910123

Balinor Books, a division of Balinor International, llc, is a boutique
publishing house domiciled in the United States.

Enjoy these other fine works from Balinor Books, now available at Amazon.com!

The Continuing Adventures of Sir Roderick Melrose
A titillating erotic romance and humorous travel adventure in the Victorian vernacular

The Conversational Poet
Love, wit and wisdom celebrated in the joy of verse

A Little Jaunt through Scandinavia, or
Norman and Lisa's Nordic Adventure in The Year of Our Volvo 2001

Mrs. Hensworthy's Bookcase
A Tale of Science Fiction, Served with Tea and Biscuits

About the author:

I always find it curious that these "About the Author" paragraphs are prepared in the third person; I believe everyone knows that this completely flattering and immodest description is inevitably prepared by the author himself, herself, itself, or whatever particular –self the author prefers.

That said, I try to aspire to justifying the title of "Renaissance Personage." Vocationally, I'm an entrepreneur trying to bring about exciting device-driven changes in the realm of medical care.   Avocationally, I'm an author, poet, architect, artist, cabinet-maker, musician.

Feel free to peruse *www.njbarta.com* for a peek at some of the pursuits that float my proverbial boat (although I might mention that boating is not necessarily one of those pursuits).

And please enjoy the journey!

My thanks to Nicole K for her editorial feedback, Allison K for her musical assistance on the GadgiYack theme, and Kate K for having two such wonderful kids!

MRS. HENSWORTHY'S BOOKCASE²
INTERDIMENSIONAL COMMERCE

0.625[1]

As I'm sure you recall, when last we left Mrs. Eleanora Hensworthy's living room, she had returned to enjoying her afternoon tea, after a series of events that rather rudely interrupted her routine; to wit, the substantial interdimensional rift that opened in a doorway formed by her bookcase; her dealings with the various otherworldly beings who had an interest in examining and repairing said rift; and the subsequent turmoil when the local constabulary and military contingents decided to get involved, and happened to destroy her kitchen (as well as several very well cared for potted plants). Finally, finally, her life had settled back into its very comfortable routine, with a pleasant afternoon fire burning in the fireplace.

As you may also recall, she was enjoying just such a scenario when, of a sudden, her front door opened once more, and, after missing for over five years, her dearly departed husband

Malthorp appeared in the living room. As we've noted before, he hadn't passed on, of course; simply departed. Now, ordinarily, such an appearance would be worthy of perhaps a raised eyebrow, or a furtive look askance, but that certainly wouldn't take into consideration Malthorp's fairly unusual provenance, as an alien who first appeared in Mrs. Hensworthy's garden in rather gelatinous form.

As a shape shifter, Malthorp had assumed a reasonably normal male formation shortly thereafter (although, as a shape shifter, he introduced a certain notable improvement that, in the interests of discretion, we shall not dwell upon here). He based his human male formation primarily upon photographs and descriptions he found in the books of Mrs. Hensworthy's library. And this is how we find him today, as he now makes his appearance.

Mrs. Hensworthy turned to the door to see Malthorp standing there on the same two legs he had created when he took human form about 25 years earlier. He smiled at her.

"Why, Malthorp! You've returned! Oh, my dear, the goings-on that we've had here. How are you?! And I believe you mentioned something about molting or some such when you departed; were you successful in your endeavor? Do sit down and tell all!" Mrs. Hensworthy was, needless to say, excited to see him.

Malthorp took the nearest chair and joined Mrs. Hensworthy in front of the fire. "Eleanora, my dear, it is lovely to be back. I must say, I missed you, as well as the old cottage. I was utterly successful in my molt, thank you very much. It took me the better part of an Earth year to find the right fresh water lake in which to immerse myself for the occasion; molting unfortunately tends to generate a great deal of heat. I found a lovely body of water, I believe the local dwellers refer to it as Lake Michigan, and spent a good deal of time on the bottom of the lake until the process was complete. I'm afraid the population of creatures in the lake is now somewhat diminished; a fellow needs to eat, after all, and molting does require just a frightful amount of energy. But now I'm back, my outermost gelatinous layer no more than a memory, and I'm feeling fully refreshed! Do tell me what's transpired since I departed."

Mrs. Hensworthy proceeded to tell Malthorp all about the interdimensional rift that had opened in the doorway of the bookcase. She also related her experiences with the various off-world characters who made an appearance, particularly Brobding Measelfort, the Measeloot who was a most congenial, mmm, fellow. She finished her narration with a synopsis of the subsequent disaster introduced by one Sergeant Major DeLade Greene, who felt it necessary to destroy her kitchen in an effort to rid the planet of what he perceived to be an 'alien menace.'

Malthorp wore a concerned expression. "Oh, no, tell me they didn't harm Maurice..." As a reminder, Maurice was Mrs. Hensworthy's favorite philodendron plant.

Mrs. Hensworthy looked sad. "Yes, I'm afraid Maurice gave his all for the cause. But I now have Penelope, a young philodendron who seems quite content in the new conservatory, provided courtesy of the government in compensation for the *utter* destruction they had wrought earlier." She brightened up considerably on mention of Penelope.

Malthorp pondered the events that had occurred. "Oh, dear, I *am* sorry I missed that rift business. I would have liked to have at least visited some of my old friends on Jordalak before the rift once again evaporated." As a point of reference, Jordalak was the earthly pronunciation of Malthorp's home planet. "And you had a Measeloot visiting! Once you get past the rather disconcerting giant bedbug appearance, they are quite the measel, or rather, friendly, sort! Well, perhaps he'll visit again, and I'll have another opportunity. After all, once they know where you are, Measeloots tend not to be strangers."

1.875^2

Several Earth months later, Malthorp and Eleanora Hensworthy were once again enjoying their afternoon tea, as they often did, before a pleasant fire in the living room. They were conversing about the upcoming vegetable competition in the village when, as if to demonstrate Malthorp's omniscience, a whooshing sound made itself known, and became louder and louder. At the same time, a rift once again made an appearance in the doorway of the bookcase, a doorway that ordinarily opened to the kitchen. The Hensworthys calmly observed the proceedings with interest.

Moments later, Brobding Measelfort, Mrs. Hensworthy's favorite Measeloot, stepped through the rift.

Mrs. Hensworthy was delighted. "Why, Mr. Measelfort! How nice to see you again!" Several strange and squeaky sounds emanated from Brobding Measelfort as he pointed to what one might perceive to be an orifice of sorts on, presumably, his head.

"Oh, yes, I'm so forgetful!" Mrs. Hensworthy reached around to a handy side table, opened a drawer, drew forth a GadgiYack, and placed it in one of her nostrils. As I'm sure you recall, the GadgiYack, placed in any convenient nostril, allows a being to instantly understand any other being, or at least understand what the being is saying. As for actually *understanding* another being, that's a philosophical question for another day.

Brobding was now completely intelligible. "I'm certainly glad you retained your GadgiYack, Mrs. Hensworthy, and it's very lovely to see you as well! Regarding the GadgiYack, I wasn't supposed to leave it here on my last visit, but I suppose it can be our little secret."

Mrs. Hensworthy pointed to Malthorp. "I'd like to introduce you to my husband, Malthorp. He's actually a Jordalakian; I'm sure you two will have much to talk about! Malthorp, this is Mr. Measelfort; I apologize, I don't recall your first name, Mr. Measelfort."

As Mrs. Hensworthy spoke, Brobding Measelfort was seen to be reaching back through the rift, and rummaging through a box of some sort. He returned a moment later with another GadgiYack in his appendage, and provided it to Malthorp, who, following Mrs. Hensworthy's lead, promptly inserted it into his left nostril. Brobding seemed pleased.

"There, that's better. I'm Brobding Measelfort. It's a pleasure, Malthorp! I see you've taken the form of the indigenous species. How is it you're residing on this particular planet? It isn't part of the Trading League, or on the network of transdimensional transport tubes, and I don't recall any interdimensional links to this particular system."

Malthorp pondered the question briefly. "Well, Brobding, I'm a bit embarrassed to relate this story, but as you're a Measeloot, I'm sure you'll take it in only the most positive light."

"I was a faculty member in the Planetary Sociology Department at the Advanced Educational Center on the planet Rangus, which I'm sure you know is renowned as a citadel of higher learning. I received a grant, in conjunction with some of my esteemed colleagues, to quietly investigate the inhabitants of the Barnork system. As you know, the Barnork and Grange systems reside in separate 3-dimensional spaces that overlap in n-space, and we had identified some concern that the Grange system might be exposed to Barnork inhabitants if there were to be an interdimensional rift of any significance in this region."

"For obvious reasons, it was all very hush-hush. The planetary systems in this galactic neighborhood, at least those that are part of the Trading League, don't like the idea of unauthorized interdimensional portals being opened to less-advanced civilizations, and the anecdotal evidence indicated that the Barnork system, and in particular Barnork 3, known colloquially as Earth, was seriously behind the technological and socially-acceptable times."

"My colleagues and I were chosen because, as shape shifters, we could blend into the local population fairly easily in order to make our observations, without the local species discovering our true nature."

"Well, all was going swimmingly at first. With the full permission of the various interplanetary authorities, we introduced a very minor little interdimensional rift that opened to the planet's atmosphere, and flew in several small vessels to various points on the planet, agreeing, as an introductory visit, to meet back at the rift point in 12 planetary rotations."

"I landed quite discreetly in an area of woodland and field, near a locale the local population identified as Nara, within a larger geographic area that the locals here refer to as Japan."

"The first inhabitants I encountered seemed very friendly indeed, although they had very limited vocal skills. Even though I was in possession of a ConversaWand, their conversational style was really quite abbreviated. As I'm sure you're aware, the ConversaWand was the predecessor to this little nasal gadget you've provided, and worked reasonably well, despite the fact that one needed to allocate an appendage so as to hold the ConversaWand in a suitably functional position." Brobding nodded knowingly.

Malthorp looked pensive for a moment. "You know, I remember when the GadgiYack first came out. There was a lot of hesitation; everyone had become so accustomed to the ConversaWand, and weren't sure how to use this newfangled widget. They had that catchy jingle, didn't they? What was it again? *'If you have translation woes, try a GadgiYack up your nose, then enjoy some super prose, but don't… put it between your toes! Try GadgiYack!'* Huh! I still remember humming that tune." (A brief aside: For those interested parties, we've provided the appropriate music for The GadgiYack Jingle, coming up shortly! But right now, let's get back to Malthorp as he relates his earlier experiences on Barnork 3…)

"The next inhabitants I found were considerably more interesting from the conversational perspective, although I had to keep adjusting my shape in order to accommodate the various species I was encountering. After some lengthy interaction, I learned that the first inhabitants with whom I attempted to interact were called 'deer,' and were known for their reserved demeanor. Still, a lovely species."

"The 12 rotations came about very quickly, as this planet tends to have a fairly rapid spin, and I wrapped up my studies. I attempted to communicate with several sorts of creatures during the study period, including those that were later identified to me as 'squirrels' and 'mice.' While they were pleasant enough, only the primary species, known as 'humans,' was really very informative, except, perhaps, for one particularly talkative squirrel, who seemed to have a *great* deal to say regarding human behaviors. The humans were quite friendly overall, but, as anticipated, were extremely limited technologically, and I had my doubts as to their reaction to other intelligent species at this point in their evolution."

"I returned to my craft and took flight, prepared to return to the rift coordinates, when I discovered that the memory circuits of my craft seemed to have an issue. I no longer had the rift coordinates online! I set down once again, in what turned out to be the garden behind this dwelling, and proceeded to rummage about in the storage compartments, hoping to find a chart or other useful data, but all I found was a bunch of food wrappers, a collection of crumbs, and a travel brochure showing some beach resorts on the planet Wowserlik 3, all left by the prior user of the vessel, who obviously enjoyed snacking while en route."

"Mrs. Hensworthy made an appearance as I was hunting about in the cabin, and I used my ConversaWand to engage her in conversation. Unfortunately, I had forgotten to take on a form that would be amenable to the local species, but luckily, she seemed to take it all in stride."

Well, one thing led to another, and as I never could find that rift, I settled down in the form of 'Malthorp,' hoping that perhaps one day another rift might be opened to my dimensional turf, as they say. I suppose my colleagues departed as planned."

Brobding listened attentively. "I'm certainly glad to have stopped by, then! Perhaps you would care to use my rift to visit your colleagues again, or at the very least, send a message to them?"

Malthorp positively beamed. "That would be absolutely superb, Brobding! I appreciate the offer. A message will do for now, as it's only been a short time from their perspective. As you know, we Jordalakians tend to measure time somewhat differently given our longevity. I'll prepare a little something you might send to Rangus on my behalf when you're ready to depart."

Mrs. Hensworthy spoke up at this juncture. "Malthorp, my dear, where are our manners?! Mr. Measelfort, may we offer you a spot of tea, and perhaps a savory tidbit in accompaniment? I'm sure you'd enjoy a little refreshment after your long journey!"

Brobding made an expression that one might interpret as a smile. "Thank you, Mrs. Hensworthy, that would be wonderful! I should mention, however, the journey along a transdimensional tube and through an interdimensional rift is a fairly quick affair; because of dimensional folding, the distances to be traversed are really quite small." Malthorp nodded in agreement. Mrs. Hensworthy also nodded in agreement, even though she wasn't quite up to speed on dimensional folding.

"Well, I'll refresh our tea and morsels in any case." As she stood up to go, she glanced in the direction of the bookcase. "Oh yes, there's that rift business again. I'll just use the hallway kitchen entrance." And with that, she made for the hall adjacent to the living room. As she arrived in the hallway, she heard Brobding speaking with Malthorp, apparently relating some of the recent events that had occurred in the nearby galactic neighborhood during Malthorp's absence, but she was too far away to hear the details.

She returned shortly thereafter with a refreshed pot of tea, and a selection of tasty biscuits and cakes for all of them to enjoy.

As Brobding sipped his tea and contemplated the delightful nuances of flavor washing over his extremely sensitive palate, he mentioned to the Hensworthys, "A very interesting idea has just occurred to me."

The GadgiYack Jingle

2.708³

Chief Inspector Lentipede had a big problem on his, for lack of a better term, hands. He was residing in his office net, contemplating the issue with his new assistant, Mop.

"I tell you, Mop, we must find the source of all this druzhia passing around the planets. As you may know, druzhia is considered what we refer to as a 'managed item' on no less than 4 planets in the Trading League, and for good reason! I know it's perfectly legal in most of the system, but those 4 planets that have restrictions on it are giving us a real pain." Mop nodded his tentacles in agreement.

Malheureuse Lentipede was a Chief Inspector in the PLAnetary Security TEam and REconnaissance Division, otherwise referred to as PLASTERED. We shall refer to 'him' as 'he' for the sake of simplicity. He and his assistant MOP were from the planet Towl, which is where PLASTERED was headquartered; for those humans unacquainted with the locale, it's pronounced like 'towel.' A Towlak appears rather like a very large orange lobster that's been having a bad day, with six appendages, and two very long and sensitive tentacles rising above their four little eyes. They like to reside in net-like structures when at work, or relaxing, or just about any time they're not moving around.

As for druzhia, several planets began to grow the substance some time ago, which in Earth terms, and including the 3-dimensional space thereabouts, would be about 24 years. It's a leafy substance that, when brewed for a short period at whatever happens to be the local boiling point for H_2O, becomes a fairly tasty and somewhat stimulating beverage. On Earth, I believe the colloquial term for the brew is 'tea.' Unfortunately, druzhia, or tea, has some odd effects on the various inhabitants in this neighborhood of this particular galaxy. To further Mop's education, Chief Inspector Lentipede proceeded to describe some of the more interesting effects druzhia exhibited in the local populations.

"Listen carefully, Mop; it's important you understand what this stuff can do to our constituents. As an example, the inhabitants of Hoolit 4 were introduced to druzhia perhaps 20 of their years past, and the stimulative effects were quite disconcerting. Oh yes, I say, quite disconcerting. Many of them were seen to be racing about their dwellings and neighborhoods, and entirely backwards. Disconcerting, indeed!" Mop listened, mesmerized.

"On the Kor planets, druzhia had a positively extraordinary effect on the local populace. As you may know, the beings of Kor look like large spiny balls. Korpits, which is how one refers collectively to the inhabitants, are more or less spherical, with short appendages protruding rather symmetrically about the sphere. They seem to have eyes, and what one might interpret as ears, everywhere, in addition to no less than four orifices, each of which might qualify as a mouth."

"Well, druzhia proved to be very popular indeed on Kor, but several Kor weeks after its introduction, the locals who imbibed decent quantities of the stuff began to grow large fluffy balls of pink fur on the ends of *all* of their appendages. Well, with all that fur on all those appendages, it blocked their line of sight from all those eyes rather considerably, and they began to run into things. Let me tell you, Mop, having a large spiny ball with fluffy pink fur run into you is not something to look forward to, no indeed!" Mop vibrated with trepidation at the thought.

"On Pleebus, druzhia was first introduced through a series of parties at only the most exclusive homes. Unknown to the Pleebusites, which is how one refers to those from Pleebus, druzhia causes a certain, ahem, *particular* appendage to grow rather dramatically, and remain in a fairly turgid state for some time. While apparently not medically harmful, it caused no end of embarrassment for those Pleebusites whose appendages were affected, although Pleebusites bearing the receptive organs of the species found it all quite titillating. But perhaps you're too young to be hearing this!" Lentipede paused in his lecture on the effects of druzhia as Mop turned a brilliant yellow, and tried to recover from his excitement.

"Aside from the medical issues, some of these effects are simply not considered proper on the more conservative planets, and the brew is known to be quite addictive for certain species."

As I'm sure the reader is aware, even some humans might be said to show evidence of these addictive aspects, particularly in certain portions of the United Kingdom, and perhaps Ireland. Let's rejoin Chief Inspector Lentipede as he continues in his contemplations.

"After careful examination and consideration, I would conjecture that this is once again the work of that criminal mastermind, Farpel."

Mop's tentacles twitched from curiosity. "Farpel, Chief Inspector?"

"Yes, this definitely has the marks of a Farpel Operation." The Chief Inspector continued, "I realize you're fairly new in your position, Mop, and so you may not be aware of it, but we've been trying to catch Dearlotin Farpelmop, also known as Farpel, for hundreds of revolutions of his home planet, Kingl 5, but he always manages to give us the slip. Somehow, he's smuggling druzhia onto the four restricted planets in violation of their local laws, and it's important that we put a stop to it. We've confirmed that he's not acquiring the goods from the legal sources in this part of the galaxy, so we've been searching diligently for his illicit source of supply. So far, nothing."

"And druzhia is just one small part of his operation; he's also been known to deal in various intoxicating beverages, such as the juice from the well-known biepalfruit. On top of that, we keep closing down establishments of his that offer... I'm loath to even mention it... games of *chance*. As fast as we close them down in one dimensional territory, he opens them again in some other dimensional space. Oh, yes, this Farpel is a shrewd character, Mop, and it's up to us to outsmart him."

Mop took a moment to absorb what he had just heard about Dearlotin Farpelmop. "Do you have a plan in mind, Chief Inspector?"

Lentipede considered the question briefly. "Yes, Mop; I'm convinced Farpel is going to make a mistake soon; his luck can't hold out forever. And when he does make a mistake, we'll be there to greet him, take away his GadgiYack, and shut him down. So, we watch, Mop, and we wait."

3.125^4

Brobding Measelfort was particularly enjoying the tea served to him by the Hensworthys. "I believe you've outdone yourself, Mrs. Hensworthy; this tea is excellent! And while we're on the subject, I believe there are quite a few beings in our galactic neighborhood who might enjoy this, how did you refer to it, beverage? I've been in transdimensional tube repair for quite some time now, and have been trying to develop a way to expand my horizons, so to speak. Do you think you might be interested in engaging in a bit of commerce across the dimensional divide?"

Mrs. Hensworthy looked at her husband Malthorp, and exchanged knowing nods. "I do believe we might be able to work something out, Mr. Measelfort. I would need to investigate the manner in which we might acquire larger quantities of tea for the purpose, but I believe it definitely has promise!"

Brobding Measelfort displayed an expression that one might interpret as pleasure, if one were to be particularly astute at interpreting the expressions of Measeloots. "Well, that's wonderful, Mrs. Hensworthy! And while you're investigating the supply, I shall make some inquiries with respect to distributing your product throughout the Trading League. I'm sure there are planets that would show interest. Would it be possible for me to take a sample?"

"Of course, of course. And don't forget to steep the tea in boiling water for 3 to 5 minutes, and strain out the tea leaves before serving. I'm sure you'll find a receptive audience, Mr. Measelfort!"

Malthorp looked somewhat pensive as he listened to the discussion. "Brobding, you may want to keep in mind that not all creatures will respond positively to this beverage. I believe the inhabitants of the Calabala system have been known to react rather badly to acidic substances. I'd suggest investigating possible side effects before offering the product around."

Mrs. Hensworthy chimed in. "Oh, yes, Mr. Measelfort, I seem to remember from your last visit, that nice being, what was her name again? Oh, it was quite unusual!"

"Ah, I do recall, that assistant accompanying the team from The Center for Education in the Galactic Sciences, I believe it was Nalanalanalanalanalanala Ditt, wasn't it? I'm fairly certain that she was from the planet Calabala. They all have extremely long names of that sort. I remember attending a party on Calabala once; by the time they completed the introductions, the party was already over! If I'm not mistaken, she turned an interesting shade of purple after absorbing some tea. I'll be sure to steer clear of Calabala in discussing the opportunities for tea."

Mrs. Hensworthy provided Brobding Measelfort with a nicely sized tin of tea, and Brobding bid his farewells as he proceeded back through the rift he had created in the transdimensional transport tube, with promises to return shortly, bearing news as to the possible avenues of distribution for the beverage.

After Brobding had gone, the rift was once again closed, and the passage from the living room to the kitchen was now as open as it had always been, as it no longer contained an other-dimensional obstruction. The Hensworthys remained before the fire, considering the conversation they had just had. Malthorp spoke up.

"Well, I suppose we'll need to find a source of tea that's somewhat more robust than the local village grocer. Perhaps we can make some discreet inquiries with the staff at Waitrose or Sainsbury's."

"I think that's an excellent idea!" Mrs. Hensworthy was getting quite enthusiastic about the whole enterprise. "And in the meantime, I've made acquaintance with some of the lovely serving staff at Jenny's, and over at Betty's Café. They may have some useful sourcing information for us!"

3.958⁵

Brobding Measelfort was a Measeloot with a mission. Now that the Hensworthys had expressed interest in the tea trade, it was up to Brobding to figure out how to distribute the goods throughout the Trading League. Brobding had been working in the transdimensional transport tubes of the MITE Corporation for ages, so he certainly knew his way around the interdimensional folds that connected the various planets in this galactic neighborhood. Now he needed to meet the right local inhabitants who would be able to move some product for him.

He had a thought. His favorite first cousin, Willodig Propmeasel, ran a restaurant and catering company on their home planet of Measel. As I'm sure you recall, all the inhabitants of Measel are readily identified in two relatively straightforward ways: first, of course, is their distinctive appearance, rather resembling a large 16-legged bedbug. The second way of identifying a Measeloot was that each of them had the term "measel" somewhere in their names. Messrs. Measelfort and Propmeasel were certainly no exception. But let's get back to our story...

Brobding wasn't too keen on actually visiting Measel. He had *so* many relatives who were more than happy to tell him what was wrong in his life, or who would try to introduce him to a cute Measeloot they knew. And on that subject, there was that Kolameas Elwinkem, the petite one with those extra large appendages, who was always trying to mate with him. And he certainly didn't need *that* right now.

He sent a message to his cousin, asking him if they might meet for a chat, but Willodig replied that he was absolutely buried with work, what with the Measel Festival of Extraordinary Stalactites on the horizon; the only way they could have a discussion was if Brobding came to the restaurant.

It was the middle of the night on Measel when Brobding made his way through a transdimensional transport tube to his home turf, hoping to avoid essentially all of his annoying relatives for the time being. As you may recall, because of its slow planetary rotation, 'night' on Measel is the equivalent of 33.2 hours, for those using Earth as a reference point. In any case, Brobding proceeded to his cousin's restaurant, and quietly let himself in. And he waited.

Shortly before daybreak, Willodig entered the restaurant, and practically molted right then and there. "Brobding! I nearly tripped over you!! What are you doing here so early in the morning?! Oh, and by the way, I understand through the polanka vine that Kolameas Elwinkem is looking for you."

Brobding winced, or issued forth an expression that might be interpreted as a wince in a Measeloot. "Emoclew, Willodig! I'm fine, thanks for asking. I have a little business to discuss with you; I'm hoping you can help me. And I wish Kolameas Elwinkem would stop chasing me already. I'm just not a fan of big appendages!"

A quick aside: In a curious and fairly amazing galactic coincidence, the common Measeloot greeting 'emoclew,' when spelled phonetically based on its Measeloot pronunciation, is precisely the opposite spelling of the Earth greeting-word 'welcome' found in use in the English-speaking realms on that particular planet. Curious, indeed. But let's hear what the Measeloots have to say.

Willowdig settled in for what he hoped would be a brief discussion. "Sorry Brobding, I'm always happy to see you, but it's just a little insane around here for the next 20 or so rotations. What's on your left and/or right mind?"

Brobding pulled out the tin of tea from a satchel that accompanied him. "I'd like you to try a beverage I've discovered on a planet outside of the Trading League. Let me prepare it for you, Willodig, and then let's talk."

As Brobding created some heated H_2O in the restaurant kitchen using a small directed beam of non-ionizing electromagnetic radiation, Willowdig asked some pointed questions. "Wait a minute; did you say a planet *outside* of the League? Where did you find this stuff? And how do I know it's not going to turn me into something strange, like a gridnap?" (Just fyi, a gridnap is a snake-like creature, with horns protruding from what one might assume to be its head, and four separate tongues flitting this way and that. Other species generally don't consider the prospect of being a gridnap to be a particularly pleasant one, though gridnaps themselves don't seem to have too many complaints. But we digress.) "You remember that plant that was introduced on Measel a few revolutions ago, I think it was called a Miraggo, with those round yellow berries? And the importers claimed it would help with under-appendage odor and make your claws shine? Yea, well, the Measeloots who indulged in it are still trying to get rid of the warts!"

Brobding returned with two vessels of brewed tea. "Will you stop your worrying, Willodig! I've tried this on several occasions, and have had no ill effects. Just try it, and tell me what you think!"

Willodig looked at the tea with an expression one might interpret as concern. "You mean 'no ill effects *so far*.' Fine, I'll try it, but if I start growing horns, you're the first one to get gored!" He sipped down some tea, and waited a few moments before commenting. "Well, no horns yet. It does have a nice flavor and texture. So? If I may now inquire, what exactly is the relationship between this beverage and your favorite cousin?"

For those who are adept at interpreting the physical attributes of Measeloots, it will be clear that Brobding looked at Willodig with what could only be seen as a sarcastic expression. "Oh, I suppose that would be you now?"

Willowdig smiled. "Oh, please, you know that I'm your favorite. And if you don't tell me what I'm supposed to do with this beverage, I'm going to invite Kolameas Elwinkem to join us!"

Brobding winced once again. "All right, Willodig, anything but that! I was hoping you might have some ideas with respect to distributing this beverage throughout the Trading League. By the way, it's called 'tea' on its planet of origin."

Willodig looked thoughtful as he took another sip of tea; his expression then turned somewhat darker. No, really, quite literally, he turned somewhat darker in color, rather an unusual shade of blue. "Wait a minute... this stuff tastes almost exactly like druzhia! What are you doing with this stuff on Measel! Don't you know it's been banned here for at least ten planetary revolutions? I remember trying this stuff when we were still in larval form. In enough quantities, it supposedly makes Measeloots stupid! Oh wait, I suppose when it comes to certain of our species, I should say 'stupider.'" Willodig vibrated in a manner that other Measeloots might interpret as a chuckle. "Anyway, I remember some of my friends who really enjoyed this stuff, and all they wanted to do was sit around drinking druzhia all day and talking about inane subjects like the practical applications of differential calculus. I think it's also been banned on some other planets of the Trading League. So what *are* you doing with this stuff, Brobding?"

Brobding looked somewhat confused. "I hadn't come across that druzhia before, Willodig, and I had no idea it was banned on Measel. I just thought of it as a pleasant indulgence. I don't want to go stepping on any legal toes, mind you, but do you think there's any reasonable opportunity for this somewhere in the Trading League?"

Willodig thought about it for a few moments as he absent-mindedly sipped more tea. "Well…, assuming I don't grow any horns or warts from this stuff, I think I might know a Measeloot, who knows a Measeloot, who might know someone who can help us identify a market. Just a word of warning, though; we may be dealing with some potentially shady characters. Does that work for you, Brobding?"

Brobding looked a little concerned, but was anxious to investigate further. "Why don't you put out some feelers, Willodig? Figuratively, of course; don't actually extend any of your feelers if there's a chance they'll be injured! Anyway, try making some inquiries and see what presents itself, and then we can figure out what we want to do."

5.208^6

The planet Measel rotated fully several times before Brobding heard from his cousin Willodig. He was busy effecting a tricky repair in the wall of one of the busier transdimensional transport tubes when a small pouch on his left side buzzed. That's where he kept his Holo-CalloMatic, that allowed him to have conversations that included holographic projections. He grabbed the Holo-CalloMatic with his appendage number 12, and saw a projection of Willodig appear before him.

"Emoclew, Willodig! I was just thinking about you! Well, at least the minor short term recollection function of my left brain was moving in that general direction. What's happening?"

Willodig was busy talking with another Measeloot, something about table settings for a big shindig that was soon to take place. "And don't forget, we'll need three of the large platters of smoked gridnap for the appetizer.

And make sure it's dehorned this time, for goodness sakes! You remember what happened to the Korpit Ambassador... Oh, emoclew, Brobding. Just tying up some loose ends for a party coming up in three rotations. I heard back from my friend, and I may have someone you can talk to about distributing that tea, but I'm not sure you're going to like it."

Brobding wore a concerned expression, or about as concerned as a Measeloot can manage. "And why won't I like it, Willodig?"

His cousin hesitated before answering. "Well, I think you better let the interested party tell you himself. I gave him your contact data, and he should be reaching out to you shortly. Have a chat and see what you think. Have to run!" Brobding saw Willodig tasting some orange-colored concoction from a large pot as he disconnected.

Several hours later (at least with respect to the rotation of Measel), Brobding was finishing up his repair when his Holo-CalloMatic buzzed again. It was an unfamiliar caller. Now usually, Brobding preferred to ignore such calls; I'm sure you can understand that, given all the Holo-CalloMatic scammers trying to get you to lease a brand new particle collider, or sell you a supposedly 'lightly used' GadgiYack, which might have been placed who-knows-where. But he knew that Willodig's connection was supposed to call, so he answered the call.

Facing him, holographically speaking, was an unfamiliar creature. For those readers accustomed to Earthly beings, this creature looked something like a Great Dane, but with four extra appendages that might be considered arms.

It was a Kinglorf, and judging by its looks, probably from Kingl 5. You might remember that those particular Kinglorfs have a pouch on each side of their torsos that they can inflate with a low-density gas, allowing them to float around on planets with higher-density atmospheres, like, for instance, Kingl 5.

Brobding stared briefly at the hologram, and asked tentatively, "May I help you?"

The Kinglorf wore what might be interpreted as a wary expression, for a Kinglorf. "I understand you'd like to, uh, 'distribute' some druzhia within the Trading League." The Kinglorf used its front appendages to place the word 'distribute' in a Kinglorf's equivalent of quotes. "I may be able to help with that, for the right price."

Brobding was not yet feeling better about the call. He found the quotation marks annoying, or as annoying as a Measeloot can manage to feel. "Yes, that's right, although I've come to understand it's also called tea in some quarters. To whom do I have the pleasure of communicating?"

It was the Kinglorf's turn to answer tentatively. "Please! No names! Not on an open Holo-CalloMatic line! We need to meet. Do you have a place where we can meet discreetly?"

The small touch receptors on Brobding's appendages stood on end. He was feeling quite uncomfortable already, but Willodig had warned him that they might be dealing with some shady characters. He thought perhaps his cousin's restaurant might work after hours, when it would be empty and quiet. "I'll send you the time and location coordinates. Do let me know if they work for you."

The Kinglorf replied quietly, "If I think it's a good location, I'll make them work. I'll watch for the coordinates." With that, the Kinglorf signed off.

'Well, he's a rather abrupt creature, isn't he?' thought Brobding as he forwarded the coordinates to the strange caller.

Several Measel days later, Brobding had returned to his cousin's restaurant. It was quite late on a pleasant evening on Measel, and Brobding was awaiting the arrival of the Kinglorf to whom he was introduced several days earlier. His cousin Willodig wouldn't be joining him this evening; he was involved with some banquet associated with the Festival of Extraordinary Stalactites, being held in a one of the many impressive caves on Measel. Apparently a problem had arisen when one of the more spectacular stalactites in the cave decided to drip some of its ever-growing mineral content directly into the soup of several dignitaries in attendance. Chaos had ensued.

Brobding was quietly reconsidering the whole concept of distributing tea when the door to the restaurant opened, and much to his surprise and dismay, in walked Kolameas Elwinkem. "Brobding! Your cousin told me you might be here! It's so good to see you! Is it good to see me?"

Brobding avoided the question, and silently vowed to properly berate his cousin for this betrayal at the earliest opportunity. He couldn't help his exasperated tone as he replied, "EmOClew, Kolameas, how are you? I'm afraid I'm rather busy this evening; perhaps we could meet again soon to catch up."

"Oh, Brobding, you're always trying to duck out on me!" Kolameas giggled, linked several appendages with Brobding, and replied in a distinctly petulant voice, "I insist we have a nice chat right now, and I won't leave until we do!"

Just as Kolameas finished her annoying reply, the door opened once more, and a multi-armed Great Dane walked into the room. He stared at the occupants for a long moment.

"Who's the druzhia guy?" he asked of no one in particular.

Brobding replied hurriedly, "Ah, that would be me."

The Kinglorf looked up and down at Kolameas. "So who's the babe with the big appendages?" The Kinglorf was apparently well acquainted with Measeloot anatomy.

Brobding spoke up hurriedly. "Oh, she's no one in particular, she was just leaving."

As you might conjecture, Kolameas was not happy on hearing these words. "No one in particular! No one in particular?! Really! I am Kolameas Elwinkem, and I don't need to remain here to be insulted! I can get that just about anywhere!"

Brobding did his best to calm Kolameas as he directed her toward the door. "Please, Kolameas, this is an important business meeting. I'll explain it to you as soon as I can, but I really must speak with this other being right now." With that, he directed her through the door and into the night, and closed the door behind her. Kolameas could be heard complaining to herself rather loudly as she proceeded to walk away.

The Kinglorf was the first to speak. "I have my kid's hatchday shindig in a Measel hour, so let's get this planet rotating, so to speak. You can call me Farpel."

Brobding was relieved that Kolameas was out of the picture for the time being, and turned when the Kinglorf addressed him. "And I am Brobding Measelfort. It's a pleasure to meet you, Mr. Farpel."

"Yeah, yeah, likewise, and it's just Farpel. Tell me what you have on your minds here, Measelfort."

Brobding found Farpel to be a bit unsettling, but he proceeded with his explanation. "Well, I would like to distribute some tea, or rather, druzhia, within the Trading League, and was hoping you might be able to help me with that."

Farpel shook his long, pointed ears. "Sorry, Meas, but we can't sell the stuff on the legal planets; the current druzhia growers and distributors in the Trading League have locked up a monopoly on the legal trade, and they get really, really nasty if someone steps into their proverbial atmosphere, if you know what I mean. An associate tried it once; his GadgiYack never quite worked right after what that druzhia gang did to his nostrils." Brobding shuddered at the thought.

There was silence as Farpel considered the issue briefly. "You know, if you're feeling particularly adventurous, I happen to know that there's an underground demand for the goods on the, shall we say, less than legally receptive planets. Here on Measel, it's quietly sold through certain channels to those seeking what you might call a 'mellow vibe.' And I happen to know the Korpits get a real buzz from the stuff. There are a few planets like that, if you're up for it. By the way, what's your source? My informants tell me that the growers in the Trading League will only sell to certain captive distributors. And I do mean 'captive.'"

Brobding shuddered involuntarily once more. "Well, I happened upon a supply from a planet that's not actually part of the Trading League. As a matter of fact, the planet doesn't even have access to the transdimensional transport tubes. I happen to work on tube repair, and came across this planet when we had a brief rift in one of the tubes."

For those who can interpret Kinglorf expressions, Farpel was looking impressed. "Interdimensional smuggling; I like it."

Brobding was somewhat taken aback at this description, as he didn't consider moving tea from Earth to the Trading League planets as 'smuggling,' but he let the comment pass for the time being. He was somewhat more concerned with the description 'less than legally receptive.' "Tell me, Farpel, how much trouble can we get into if we supply tea to planets where it's been banned?"

Farpel displayed a confident air as he looked at Brobding and considered the question. "If you're going to think small, Meas, you're not going to get anywhere. The big deals involve some risk. Sure, we could be banned from the transdimensional transport tubes, we could be banished to the Whoola Planets, but that shouldn't stop you if you're serious about getting into the business. There are always ways around these things."

Brobding wasn't having a good day from the perspective of shuddering. It happened again at the mention of the Whoola Planets. He had never actually visited, but he heard the inhabitants only ate, and Brobding swallowed hard at the thought, *vegetables* there. He wasn't sure he'd survive an ordeal like that.

Farpel could see that Brobding was having second thoughts. "Listen, Meas, stop worrying about all the possible downsides, and let's talk about the upsides. A variety of beings really want this stuff, and are willing to pay for it, and from what I've seen, it doesn't do anybody any harm; they just get their particular special buzz from using it. Besides, I've been playing this game for quite a while, and you don't see me having to chow down on plants all the time. Give it a shot!"

Brobding thought for a few moments. He *was* getting *really* bored just effecting Tube repairs, and wanted to try something new. Besides, he liked Farpel's positive attitude. He managed to muster some enthusiasm in his tone as he replied, "All right, Farpel, we'll give it a try!"

6.250[7]

Brobding Measelfort was trying to be a patient Measeloot. He had heard from Farpel a short time after their conversation at the restaurant of Brobding's cousin Willodig; Farpel wanted to meet 'the supply,' to make sure he wasn't wasting his time aligning distribution channels with subsequently nothing to distribute.

As a result, Brobding made another interdimensional visit through Mrs. Hensworthy's bookcase, and arranged a little gathering. He was residing in the Hensworthy's living room, awaiting Farpel's arrival. He wasn't sure how Farpel was going to actually arrive, given that Farpel didn't like using the transdimensional transport tubes, but Farpel promised that he would attend, so Brobding waited, enjoying a cup of tea in the interim.

Sure enough, the Earth had rotated through about 14 degrees of arc when, of a sudden, an interdimensional rift opened in the middle of the Hensworthy's living room ceiling, Farpel dropped through the rift, and he slowly floated to the floor. Please recall that those Kinglorfs from Kingl 5 can float around on planets having a high density atmosphere, simply by inflating the pouches on each side of their torsos with a low-density gas.

Brobding appeared confused; he wasn't aware of any transdimensional tubes running in the vicinity of the Hensworthy's living room ceiling, and if anyone knew about transdimensional transport tubes, it was Brobding Measelfort. "Greetings, Farpel. Allow me to introduce you to the Hensworthys. And before we go further, I'm curious: how did you manage to arrive without accessing the transdimensional tubes, and for that matter, arrive in that particular locale?"

Farpel looked smug, for a Kinglorf, as he replied, "Oh, *that*; well, for various business and personal reasons, I don't use the transdimensional tubes. I prefer to travel through micro-folds in an alternative n-space."

A little important background might be useful here. Before he turned to a life of questionable and/or hedonistic pursuits, Farpel had been an enthusiastic and promising young student of Lorkin Lort, renowned Professor of Multidimensional Physics at Lechien 7's Center for Education in the Galactic Sciences. As I'm sure you remember, Professor Lort was one of the key figures in mapping the interdimensional folds that formed the very foundation of the transdimensional transport network. This of course brought to life the MITE Corporation, which maintains the current network of transdimensional transport tubes, and allowed commerce to move from one planet to another with essentially the same ease as travelers had earlier enjoyed in moving from town to town on their own planets.

Under Professor Lort's tutelage, Farpel learned all about multidimensional folds. His education went well past the theoretical, however, as he delved into the practical aspects of addressing both different subsets of n-space, and the functionality of interdimensional folding within those subsets. But back to our story.

Brobding couldn't help himself; he had to interject before proceeding with the introductions. "But, in the interest of dimensional stability, the Trading League has banned the use of unauthorized interdimensional folds in an alternative n-space for transit among planets."

Farpelmop replied, "Yeah, well, I don't necessarily recognize the authority of the Trading League to stop me." He chuckled noticeably.

Mrs. Hensworthy spoke up. "Oh, I like this one." She sensed that the conversation might be getting a bit heated between Messrs. Measelfort and Farpel (or at least as heated as a conversation can get when a Measeloot is involved), and so decided to resume the introductions on her own. "Mr. Farpel, I'm Eleanora Hensworthy, and this is my husband Malthorp. He happens to be a Jordalakian."

Farpel looked them over for a moment, and eyed Malthorp with some suspicion, as Jordalakians were known to be scrupulously ethical, and certainly too scrupulously ethical for Farpel's taste. "Good to meet you, but what exactly is a Jordalakian doing on this backwater planet?"

The Hensworthys chose to ignore the 'backwater planet' comment in the interests of diplomacy. Malthorp chimed in, "Ah, just a small navigational accident some time ago, sir. I assure you, nothing nefarious."

Farpel decided to continue for the moment; he could determine Malthorp's perspective on this trading business when the time was right. "Right, let's talk druzhia, or *tea*, as I understand it to be called here. What's the plan from the supply side? I don't want to be calling in favors to move the stuff if we can't get it in the first place."

The Hensworthys looked at each other, and Mrs. Hensworthy spoke up. "Well, dear, we've spoken with a lovely local tea shoppe, and they've agreed to partner with us so that we can have a plentiful supply of tea in exchange for a bit of commission on the sale. Just out of curiosity, how much tea do you think you might be able to sell on those planets Mr. Measelfort had mentioned; what was that again, the Trading League?"

Farpel had done his own bit of homework before coming to this little gathering, and had a pretty good idea what demand looked like on the so-called 'forbidden' planets when it came to tea distribution. "I added up the values from my contacts; Meas, do you know the units of mass they happen to use in this place?"

Fortunately, Brobding had an earlier side conversation with Mrs. Hensworthy on this very subject. "Well, given the gravity parameters on this planet, I can work out the mass conversions and local weight equivalents if you give me the mass values in Vippels."

Farpel thought for a moment. "I checked out the rotation and revolution schedule on this place before I got here, so in local numbers, I think we can move about 4.2^{12} Vippels of druzhia for each planetary revolution, for starters."

Brobding's brow, or its equivalent in his case, furrowed as he did some quick calculations. "I think I have it; Mrs. Hensworthy, to put that in weight terms I understand to be in common use here, that works out to about 1,733 of your kilograms of tea during the first planetary revolution, or as you refer to it, 'year,' of sales."

Mrs. Hensworthy looked like she was about to fall out of her chair. "SEVENTEEN HUNDRED KILOGRAMS, did you say?!"

In a calm tone, Brobding quickly corrected the figure. "That would be 1,733 actually, Mrs. Hensworthy."

Now it was Mrs. Hensworthy's turn to have a furrowed brow. She shot Brobding a look that suggested the exact figure was not really the point of her reaction, and dwelled on the figure briefly, before she replied in a somewhat exasperated fashion, "Well, I can see that I'll need to make some further arrangements with respect to our supply!"

There was a brief silence before Farpel chimed in. "Do you think we might, ah, sample the goods? I'd like to know that we're offering quality stuff."

Mrs. Hensworthy had by that time recovered from her shock as to the quantities of tea to be required for this venture. "Oh, yes, we are being the neglectful hosts." Malthorp stood before Mrs. Hensworthy had a chance to react further. "I'll get the tea together, dear; I can see you're still absorbing the rather large supply figure." With that, he disappeared into the hallway and moved toward the kitchen.

After Malthorp had gone, Mrs. Hensworthy turned back to Farpel. "Tell me, Mr. Farpel, have you been in this business long?"

Farpel's smile was noticeable, even to a human, especially considering that Kinglorfs had 200 rather squared-off teeth arrayed in two rows. "Lady, in your planetary terms, I've lived 427 revolutions so far, and I've been in all kinds of businesses. This is nothing new to me. Of course, this time is a little different, what with a supply source outside the Trading League, but I'm confident we can make it work. It actually makes it kind of interesting."

Brobding had that furrowed brow again. "I suppose you're going to use an alternative subset of n-space for pick-up and deliveries."

Farpel looked a little surprised that Brobding would even bring that up. "You better believe it, Meas. If we try to move those kinds of goods through the transdimensional transport tubes, we're going to attract a lot of attention.

And given where we'll be selling the goods, we really don't want a lot of attention, now, do we?"

Farpel's response did nothing to relax Brobding's furrow; Farpel couldn't resist addressing Brobding's concern.

"RELAX, Meas, will you?! We have nothing to worry about. I've got the interdimensional folds down to a science, so to speak, and can open micro-rifts pretty much wherever we need them, for both pickup and delivery. So stop worrying, and enjoy the ride!"

Brobding Measelfort did his best to relax. The furrow finally subsided, at least for the time being.

Malthorp returned with a tray containing the various goods needed to serve a proper cup of tea, as well as some biscuits and cakes. "A spot of druzhia, anyone?"

7.292^8

It had been four months since the Hensworthy household initiated its interdimensional tea business, and sales were moving along swimmingly. At first, a steady stream of delivery vans arrived at the Hensworthy cottage, dropping huge boxes containing tins of tea, but then the neighbors started to complain, and something had to be done about it.

Subsequently, Mrs. Hensworthy had a nice little chat with the tea distribution warehouse, located on the outskirts of London. She arranged for them to place the tea in a storage container located in their parking lot, with the understanding that she would retrieve the tea on a regular schedule. Unbeknownst to the tea distributor, Farpel was opening a small interdimensional rift directly in the closed container, and had some of his hench-Kinglorfs move the tea through an interdimensional fold to a warehouse he maintained in an alternate 3-space. Neat, clean, and untraceable.

Demand was brisk on the various planets where druzhia was officially banned, and the local populations seemed to really enjoy having access to this 'forbidden fruit.' As an example, productivity was *way* up on Hoolit 4 thanks to the stimulative effects of this magic elixir; with more productivity, manufacturing and sales of all sorts of products increased, with a commensurate improvement in tax revenues for the local governments. While government officials were certainly pleased at this, they were concerned about the sudden influx of a substance that was considered illicit on their planet, and were really concerned as to its source, as it wasn't coming through the transdimensional transport tubes. They were in a quandary.

Barabing Weekel Malamoosh, Chief Controller of one of the larger population districts on Hoolit 4, convened what one might refer to as an 'intimate' meeting with two of his fellow District Controllers to discuss the issue.

"Fellow Hoolitans, we have an interesting problem before us. On the one appendage, we have a great deal of druzhia arriving on Hoolit 4 from points unknown, which is absolutely sucking guaackles out of the ordinary economy to pay for the stuff. On the other appendage, we're collecting even *more* guaackles in tax receipts because of the increased productivity we're seeing, what with all that stimulation from the druzhia. What to do, what to do. Thoughts?"

Sintower Fromm Palawak, a Controller from one of the smaller districts, chimed in, in a rather petulant tone, for a Hoolitan. "Well, it *is* illegal, after all! Shouldn't we be addressing this with PLASTERED, or one of the other security groups that service the Trading League? I mean, why should *we* expend our own resources trying to rein this in? Isn't it their job?"

Barabing considered the comment for a moment. "I think the real question, Sintower, is, do we want to rein this in at all? Legality aside, we're practically swimming in guaackles because of the stimulative effects, and that's not going to hurt us at election time, either." The other two Controllers clicked in agreement.

As one of the more astute members of the Controller Council, Billpouder Freez Kowdingding had been listening attentively to this exchange; it was time for him to offer his two guaackles' worth on the subject. "I have a suggestion, if I may." Barabing signaled for Billpouder to proceed. "As we don't want to condone a violation of our esteemed laws, I would suggest we ask PLASTERED to look into this druzhia business; given their bureaucracy, that will take quite some time. Meanwhile, I don't see that we need be overly cooperative in the investigation. If the security beings happen to find something interesting, that's their business. In the meantime, we publicly lament this druzhia scourge, so as to ensure the public of our law-abiding nature, while quietly accepting the benefits it has chosen to bestow upon us. Who knows? By the next election cycle, the ruling body may choose to legalize the annoying weed anyway."

The other Controllers nodded in agreement; there were smiles all around the table. No, quite literally all around the table, since Hoolitans have oral orifices that are tremendously wide by human standards.

Thanks to interdimensional folding in an alternate n-space, Farpel was able to drop quantities of tea each Earth week, in many locations on the various planets, without anyone being the wiser. He had an established network in place on each planet to create a retail channel for the goods. He did have one small problem with which to contend, however. Farpel dropped out of Mrs. Hensworthy's ceiling one day to discuss the issue, but before he could broach the subject, Mrs. Hensworthy opened the conversation.

"Mr. Farpel, I appreciate your visit. I must tell you, this tea is getting quite expensive, and I really need to be receiving some value from you, from the sales, that is, if we're going to pay our suppliers!"

"Well, lady, we're moving the goods well enough, with what you might call 'satisfying' cash flow. The problem I have is, I'm receiving payment in the local currencies. Now I can deal with the currency translations within the

Trading League planets well enough; I'm paying Meas, you know, Brobding Measelfort, in spunod, the current currency on Measel, but I have no idea what you creatures use as currency on this planet. If you can deal with guaackles, korpitwinkies, storts, or spunod, we have no problem. Otherwise, you need to tell me what the conversion is to your means of exchange."

The Hensworthys considered the issue for a few moments, and Malthorp had a thought. "Well, Mr. Farpel, we really don't have exchange rates for those currencies here on Earth, but perhaps you could convert our share of the proceeds into something more tangible."

Farpel paused, and gave him a look. "For example?"

Malthorp had a few suggestions. "Gold or diamonds come to mind, if you're acquainted with those substances. We have a human, known as a jeweler, in a town nearby who might be able to help us move either of those items into the local currency."

"Diamonds? Really? On Pleebus, those are considered bright, shiny toys for kids, but if that's what you want, I should be able to buy them with storts, the planetary currency, without arousing much suspicion. I'll just tell them I'm running some kids' birthday parties."

"On a different subject, I assume your supplier hasn't caught on to my interdimensional rift in his container yet?"

Mrs. Hensworthy wore a smile as she replied, "No, thankfully, he seems to think we're arriving by truck each week to pick up our supplies. By the by, Mr. Farpel, perhaps you could explain to me exactly how that little rift trick of yours works. Mr. Measelfort told us that you're using the same approach to deliver the tea on the various planets."

It was Farpel's turn to smile. "Yea, I learned a few things in my youth that have proven to be tremendously helpful in, shall we say, circumventing the conventional channels of commerce. It's quite simple, Mrs. Hensworthy." Farpel went to the desk in the living room, and picked up a pad of paper residing there. "Imagine this as a collection of more-or-less two-dimensional planes. Now the beings living on one plane can't see beings on another plane, because, well, they're two-dimensional and don't have any perception across the dimensional divide separating *this* 2-space from *this* 2-space." As he spoke, he pointed to one page, and then another. "But now a 3-space being comes along." He selected a letter opener resting in a cup on the desk, and drove it through several sheets of paper. "And WOINK! The 3-spacer not only perceives all these 2-space regions, but has just transitioned across them."

"I do the same thing, only I'm operating in an encompassing n-space region, and moving interdimensionally at sections where the 3-space regions intersect. Since the various 3-spaces are completely enveloped within the n-space, the intersections are essentially infinite. So I choose where I want to transition from one 3-space into another 3-space, and WOINK! There I am. There are also 4-spaces out there, but I usually avoid them. First, they give me a headache, and second, the beings in 4-space regions have a kind of annoying superiority complex."

Mrs. Hensworthy nodded knowingly, although she still felt a little fuzzy on the subject. "Thank you, Mr. Farpel, that was most enlightening. Is there anything else we might do for you today, while you're visiting?"

"No, I think that covers it. I'll be visiting Pleebus shortly, and will be sure to get you some diamonds while I'm there." And with that, Farpel inflated his pouches, rose to the ceiling of the living room, and disappeared through the interdimensional rift he had created there. The rift then closed behind him, and the ceiling looked as it always did, a flat more-or-less 2-dimensional construct, with a bit of very nice dentil crown molding around the edges.

8.125^9

Chief Inspector Lentipede was in a quandary. He was sitting in the net in his office, discussing the situation with his assistant, Mop, and a bright new rookie investigator named Kerolirolia Sharboff, who happened to be a Chienolian. As I'm sure you recall, the Chienolians were usually from Lechien 7, as was our new investigator; in the interest of brevity, we shall refer to her simply as Sharboff.

Although, come to think of it, there were also some Chienolians from Lechien 6, but only those who enjoyed really *really* hot weather, as Lechien 6 was considerably closer to the star presiding over that particular system. On the other hand, the Chienolians on Lechien 7 were often heard to complain that they felt cold, so the whole star system was rather a losing proposition from the weather perspective.

I probably don't need to remind you that the system was named 'Lechien' supposedly because, without the advantages of a GadgiYack, the inhabitants sounded like yapping dogs when they spoke. The planet has also been called the Annoying Yorkie Planet for the same reason, although I have it on good authority that the locals on Lechien 7 consider that particular moniker as rather insulting. But let's get back to our story.

Chief Inspector Lentipede was discussing some new feedback he had received regarding recent incidents on several planets, due to the virtual epidemic of druzhia use.

"It's absolutely astonishing, I tell you. Druzhia seems to be simply dropping out of the atmosphere onto these planets! And as soon as we identify one point of entry for the stuff, another one opens somewhere else!"

Lentipede continued, waving his tentacles in frustration. "I just received a call from an acquaintance about a recent election held on Pleebus. I'm sure you two remember that druzhia causes certain, shall we say, unusual occurrences of turgidity in certain portions of the Pleebusites, changes that I probably shouldn't be discussing in multi-species company!   My acquaintance was telling me that, as a result, relations have improved so dramatically among the, for lack of a better term, males and females of the species that the election had only a two percent turnout of the population; everyone was simply too busy enjoying each other to bother voting!"

"And I'm getting these frantic holo-calls from some of the local constabulary. Here's a call from the Kor planets I received just this morning."   He touched a panel, and a holographic image appeared before them.   It was a Korpit, jumping up and down rather excitedly, and speaking in a fairly desperate tone from one of her orifices.

"It's a madness, an absolute madness here! Korpits are rolling all around town, covered in fluffy pink fur, and making funny squeaking noises as they move about! I was practically run over by two of them just today! And when they come down from their infernal druzhia high, they shed all that pink fur, and it's forming great balls of the stuff, and blowing all over the place! It's like a scourge... we can't get away from it, I tell you! We're getting buried in this stuff! Pink fur everywhere... You've got to do something! You've got to do something about it NOW!" The rest of her diatribe was substantially muffled as a large cloud of fluffy pink fur drifted by, obscuring the holographic image of the caller; she then disconnected.

Lentipede allowed a few moments for his associates to consider what they had just seen. "Well...thoughts?"

Mop and Sharboff sat in silence for a moment longer, and Mop spoke up. "Well, Chief Inspector, that looks pretty bad, from the fluffy pink fur perspective. Perhaps we should have someone on the ground there, to see if we can at least hunt down some of the druzhia suppliers on Kor."

Sharboff had a thought in that regard. "Excuse me, Chief Inspector, but do we have any Korpits here at PLASTERED? If so, perhaps we could mount an undercover operation to follow up on Mop's suggestion."

Lentipede looked a little sad. "We had two Korpits on staff not long ago. Unfortunately, a heavy wind came up during some training exercises. The Korpits caught the breeze, and proceeded to roll over five of our other agents. We had to let them go; not enough wind resistance."

Lentipede contemplated the situation briefly. "Sharboff, I think you'll need to be our Chienolian on the ground on Kor."

Sharboff and Mop were both somewhat taken aback, and Sharboff reacted first. "But Chief Inspector, I'm fairly new at this, and Mop has a lot more experience! Do you really think it should be me?"

Lentipede nodded his tentacles. "Yes, you're elected, Sharboff. First, the atmosphere on Kor is closer to Lechien 7 than it is to Towl, Mop's home planet, and you Chienolians are renowned for your flexibility when it comes to dealing with planetary atmospheres. Second, if a Towlak shows up on Kor, it's going to raise a lot of suspicion; Kor and Towl are notorious trading rivals. The Korpits will think a Towlak is there to steal trade secrets, which means, due to the lack of trust, a Towlak isn't going to learn anything from the Korpits."

"You're the ticket, Sharboff. We'll need to give you a good cover story, of course. Let's think about that, and reconvene tomorrow."

The evening passed quickly, and the group was back in Lentipede's office the following morning.

Lentipede started right in on the conversation as he prepared his morning cup of druzhia. The other two were looking at him rather quizzically. "What?? Druzhia is perfectly legal here on Towl! Listen, we just uphold the laws, we don't make them. In any case, let's get back to something important."

"I did some investigating of my own last night. I found that an enterprising company on Kor has been gathering the fluffy pink fur that's now to be found virtually everywhere, and is manufacturing pink fur coats. Given you Chienolians are always complaining about the cold anyway, I thought this could be a perfect cover for you, Sharboff. You're going to be a Chienolian entrepreneur looking to import fluffy pink fur coats to Lechien 7. You should start with the pink fur coat manufacturers; maybe they know something. Take the transdimensional transport tubes to the Kor system tomorrow, and report back with your findings."

Although Sharboff found the 'always complaining about the cold' comment somewhat condescending, she kept her thoughts on the subject to herself to humor her boss, and departed for home to prepare for her journey to Kor.

As she walked out of the meeting, she could hear Lentipede calling after her, "...and do try to get a lead on the whereabouts of that Farpel!"

9.375^{10}

"Well, Sharboff, what have you found?" Kerolirolia Sharboff had returned from her assignment on Kor, and Chief Inspector Lentipede had reconvened a meeting with her and his assistant Mop to discuss the findings.

"Did you manage to get any leads on the whereabouts of that nogoodnik Farpel?" Lentipede was chomping at the proverbial bit for feedback. "Nice fur coat, by the way."

As she walked into Lentipede's office, Sharboff was wearing the fluffiest, most extraordinarily pink fur coat ever to be seen in the local galactic neighborhood. It was so very pink that it practically glowed in the dark. Sharboff was rather surprised that the Chief Inspector even noticed.

"Thank you, Chief Inspector! I do have some interesting items to report. Per your instructions, my first stop was FuzzBounce, the outerwear company on Kor that's gathering all that pink fur to make coats. I met directly with Pradona Fweebic, the Executive Golgot of FuzzBounce, and the Korpit who's manufacturing the goods. She told me that there's an old Korpit saying: 'If life gives you fluffy pink fur, then make fluffy pink fur coats.' Since I was posing as a possible distributor, she gave me a free sample!"

Lentipede smiled rather sadly, for a Towl. "I'm sorry, Sharboff, but that coat was received in the line of duty; it's the property of PLASTERED now." Seeing Sharboff's crestfallen expression, he quickly continued, as he didn't see any good reason to demoralize the troops. "However, I think it would be perfectly acceptable for you to continue to test its various qualities, and prepare a detailed evaluation on that, at least until the fur starts falling out." Sharboff once again wore a broad smile, and continued to relate the happenings on Kor.

"I questioned Pradona Fweebic to determine if she had any relationship with Dearlotin Farpelmop, but she didn't even recognize the name. It seems her only link to this case involved the gathering of pink fur. Apparently, the planetary government even gave her some sort of a grant, since she was doing her part to clear up the planet-wide fluffy pink fur situation."

"On a hunch, I did make some inquiries with several of the local constabularies, to see if they had received reports of any unusual characters appearing in their jurisdictions, and I came across the most extraordinary thing. It seems someone matching the description of Farpelmop was seen in several of the jurisdictions, and according to the reports, was seen in four different jurisdictions at exactly the same time! And from what I saw in the data, this happened at least three different times."

"And then, in the most amazing coincidence, I thought I saw someone that looked like Farpelmop myself! I tried to investigate further, but before I reached the location where I thought I had seen the suspect, an extremely large ball of pink fur rolled in front of me and obscured my view. By the time the pink fur had passed by, the suspect was gone."

Lentipede's tentacles twitched with excitement. "That *is* interesting, Sharboff! It's a shame you had that pink fur obstruction foil your pursuit of the suspect, though. Let me tell you, when pink fur gets in the way of our investigations, it's really time to do something about this."

"While you were engaged on Kor, we were doing a little investigating of our own. Mop, bring up those sighting reports that we received, and let's compare them to Sharboff's data."

The team stared intently at the data projected in the atmosphere in front of them, and Mop was the first to observe something exciting. "Look at *that*! Here, at time point 42:27:04:16 on Kor, there were also two simultaneous sightings reported on Pleebus of someone bearing Farpel's description! And look, here are another three on Measel at the same time!"

Lentipede sat back in his net, and pondered the data. "Extraordinary; absolutely extraordinary. But how can that be? He can't be in 9 places at once!"

The group contemplated the possibilities in silence for a while, and Mop spoke up with a suggestion. "I realize this is just a wild idea, Chief Inspector, but perhaps Farpel is introducing holograms of himself in some way, in different places at the same time."

Lentipede thought about it for a moment, and nodded his tentacles. "Well, Mop, it's an interesting thought, but I don't think that's quite it."

They considered the problem for several moments longer, and then Lentipede sprang up excitedly. "I've got it! It must be that he's using 3-dimensional imaging to show up in several locations at once!"

Mop looked at the Chief Inspector for a moment, before replying with enthusiasm, "That must be it, Chief Inspector!"

Sharboff, the rookie investigator, looked at them both as if they had lost their multiple minds. "But Mop just said…"

Lentipede interrupted her. "Now, now, Sharboff, do try to keep up with us; I'm sure you can learn something here." Sharboff shook her tentacles in disbelief, but figured she'd be better off keeping her orifice closed.

Lentipede thought about the implications of multi-dimensional imaging in multiple locations. "Farpel would either need accomplices to project the images simultaneously, or have holo-projectors set up in various places. But if it was the latter, the images should always appear in the same places, unless he keeps moving the projectors. Let me see that data again." The group perused the data carefully, although, at this point, Mop and Sharboff weren't sure what they were looking for.

After a careful review, Lentipede could only reach one conclusion. "Look at that... according to the data, Farpel never appears in a given place more than once. I think we can therefore safely conclude that he must have a bunch of hench-creatures assisting him with these holo-projections."

"Tell me, Sharboff, did you gather any intelligence on where the supplies are coming from, or how they're being delivered to the Korpit population?"

"Yes, Chief Inspector! I decided to interview some of the known druzhia users; they weren't hard to find. First, there are a *lot* of Korpits who seem to be using druzhia, and second, of course, is all that pink fur on their appendages. I met with several, and waited until they started to molt pink fur, so I'd be sure that their multiple brains could focus on my inquiries."

"Good thinking, Sharboff!" Lentipede was impressed.

"It turns out, the stuff is being sold to them in plain sight! They all told me the same story: they would be rolling around in a Korpit shopping mall, and suddenly they would come across one of those pop-up kiosks; you know, the kind selling silly doodads, or those cheap particle colliders. Only this time, the kiosk was selling druzhia! And when I say pop-up, I mean pop-up. In each case, according to my witnesses, the kiosk would appear out of nowhere, make a bunch of sales, and then disappear the same way."

Lentipede fell back in his net. "How? How is he doing that?! I think there's more to this Farpel than meets the visual cortices."

"Good work, Sharboff. This is really useful stuff. I'd like you to interface with the constabulary on Pleebus, and see if you can corroborate Farpel's mode of operation."

"In the meantime, Mop, I think you should do some homework on Dearlotin Farpelmop; maybe we can get some insight into how he's accomplishing these seeming acts of magic with this druzhia."

Several days later (at least, several days from the perspective of a Towlak), Mop reported back to the team with his findings on Farpel.

"Well, Chief Inspector, I've made some interesting discoveries." The tentacles on both Lentipede and the rookie Sharboff bobbed in anticipation. "First, I decided to do a search on a range of data sources for permutations on the name Dearlotin Farpelmop. I don't know if you're aware of it, Chief Inspector, but the Kinglorfs often name their children based on variations of a relative's name."

Lentipede looked annoyed. "Of *course* I knew that, Mop! Even a rookie like Sharboff here knows the basics on these species." In actuality, Lentipede had no idea that Kinglorfs had such naming conventions, but he wasn't about to admit that to an underling. "What were you hoping to find with these permutations?"

"Well, sir, I thought that perhaps we might connect with one of Farpelmop's relatives, and they might possibly have some insight as to his whereabouts. As it turns out, I found one 'Loteardin Popfarmel' in the enrollment registries of the Center for Education in the Galactic Sciences on Lechien 7." As a Chienolian, Sharboff's four ears perked up noticeably on mention of her home world. "There was also a Readolint Marfolpep who showed up as a member of a knitting club on the planet Wokwok Thirdinline, but from what I could find, I don't think she has any relationship to Farpelmop."

"Getting back to the student Popfarmel, it seems he was enrolled in his youth as a Multidimensional Physics major under the instruction of Professor Lorkin Lort."

Lentipede's tentacles were positively vibrating now. "I've heard of that Lort fellow! I seem to recall reading somewhere that the transdimensional transport tubes came about as a result of his findings, or something along those lines. So Mop, do you think this Popfarmel is somehow related to the infamous Dearlotin Farpelmop?"

"I think it could certainly be a possibility, Chief Inspector. As a next step, I would like to suggest we question this Professor Lort, and see if he remembers anything about Popfarmel that might be useful."

Lentipede was encouraged. "Good, good! Why don't you contact him, Mop, and arrange a holo-call with the fellow. Excellent! I feel like the trail is getting warmer. In the meantime, Sharboff, did you find out anything useful from our friends on Pleebus?"

Sharboff turned an interesting shade of purple. "Well, it's just a little embarrassing, Chief Inspector. According to the local authorities with whom I interacted, it seems like the Pleebusites afflicted with druzhia addiction can't seem to get out of their bedrooms long enough to get any work done. The local governments are starting to complain on two fronts. First, tax revenues are down because a measurable portion of the population is neither working nor spending their storts, which, as you know, is the currency on Pleebus. And secondly, the government officials are worried about a population explosion, with all this, shall we say, bedroom activity going on! They're seriously worried that druzhia is going to destabilize their economy."

"As for the mode of operation, from what I could gather, it's pretty much identical to what's happening on Kor. Pop-up druzhia kiosks show up out of nowhere, get mobbed by Pleebusites desperate for the goods, and then simply disappear."

Lentipede shook his tentacles. "Well, it's just got to stop, that's all there is to it. Mop, get on to that fellow Lort, and let's hope he can provide some useful insight into this mess. In the meantime, Sharboff, see if we have a hologram of Farpelmop in our files. If we do, I'd like you to start distributing the image throughout the Trading League planets, and we'll see if anyone else has seen this character recently."

10.417[11]

Lorkin Lort was in a good mood as his holo-call connected to PLASTERED Headquarters. He remembered the student Popfarmel quite well indeed, and was pleased to have a discussion on the subject with Chief Inspector Lentipede and his associates.

Lentipede took the call excitedly. "Greetings, Professor Lort. Thank you for taking the time to discuss with us this important subject."

"Not at all, not at all. I presume you are Chief Inspector Lentipede?"

"Indeed, a pleasure to meet you, Professor. These are my associates, Mop and Sharboff. We'd like to ask you a few questions about a student under the name of Popfarmel who apparently studied under you quite some time ago. Do you recall the student by any chance?"

Lorkin Lort responded with a smile, "Oh, yes, Chief Inspector, I remember Popfarmel quite well, quite well indeed. One of my best students, actually. I seem to recall he's a Kinglorf; They're quite a bright species, as a rule."

"As you know, Kinglorfs have those unusual sacks they can inflate, and I remember that Popfarmel used to blow them up and absent-mindedly float around the class as he contemplated a particularly tricky multidimensional physics problem. It was all rather distracting to the other students, of course. But I'm sure you realize that, with multi-species classes, we must try to be accommodating to these little species-related idiosyncrasies."

"Yes, Popfarmel took a very strong interest in multidimensional physics; as a matter of fact, I had high hopes that he would continue in his studies and join the Professorial Union. Alas, he departed after graduating top of his class, and I lost track of him."

"Tell me, Professor, do you recall if Popfarmel had any particularly close friends or relatives with whom he had contact while enrolled?"

The left and right side of Lort's torso wrinkled noticeably, indicating that he was deep in thought. "No, no, he seemed to be rather a loner, to tell you the truth. Studying, studying, studying. A very dedicated student."

"Were there any particular areas of interest that Popfarmel was pursuing as one of your students, Professor?"

Lort turned to a device next to him. "I may have some of his work on file; I do try to retain the best of my students' work. Let me just check my records....yes, here it is. Popfarmel wrote quite an interesting treatise entitled *Addressing Physicality Implications within the context of Interdimensional Folding in an Alternative n-Space: Practical Applications*. I thought it offered some exciting insights as an extension of my own work on the subject."

"Oh, dear, you don't think...I mean, he didn't actually try to apply this to alternative n-space, did he? As I'm sure you know, at my recommendation, the Trading League has seriously discouraged any activities in alternative n-spaces, due to the possible interdimensional instabilities that can be introduced. Oh dear! Oh my! If Popfarmel has actually implemented some of the concepts presented in his treatise, well, there could be serious repercussions with respect to matter and atmospheric transfer, as well as gravitational perturbations across dimensional domains. Oh dear!" Lort was getting quite disturbed at the prospect of uncontrolled interdimensional rifts across n-space.

Lentipede knew he was on the right track. "Tell me, Professor, just how would these interdimensional thingamabobs you're talking about manifest themselves?"

Lort thought about it for a moment. "Well, Chief Inspector, in the most likely scenario, a two-dimensional portal would open, providing the opportunity for transition between dimensional spaces. The portal could be anywhere from a miniscule micron-sized rift to an opening on a planetary scale. If it were to be a very large rift, however, gravitational disturbances would be very likely in the vicinity of the rift, given a sudden introduction of matter from one r-space to another, where r is greater than or equal to 3. In a similar vein, with virtually any rift, there would be noticeable energy fluctuations in the same vicinity, based on the energy differential between the newly joined domains, although, ceteris paribus, the energy fluctuations would be more or less proportional to the size of the rift."

"I'm sorry, Professor, I don't speak Chienolian, but I get your meaning. So, potentially, we could detect these rifts by detecting energy fluctuations, is that correct?"

"Yes, Chief Inspector, that is theoretically possible, but you would need to look for the unique energy signatures that differentiate the rift fluctuations from the noise of existing energy fluctuations in your r-space. In other words, you need to look for the energy signature outliers."

Thank you, Professor; that's very interesting. Do you think you might give our technical people some insight into building the appropriate gear to detect these fluctuations?"

Lort became excited. "Yes, that would be quite interesting! But it's important that you have some idea where a rift may be about to occur; just searching generally across an r-space would be a stupendously challenging task."

Now it was Lentipede's turn to get excited, but he restrained himself for the moment. "Before I forget, Professor, do you recall what Popfarmel looked like?"

Lort was briefly lost in thought, but quickly came back to the conversation. "Oh, yes, well, of course; he was a typical Kinglorf. You know, large head, four legs and four forward appendages, those curious pouches on each side of the torso. I seem to recall that Popfarmel had a distinctive mark on one side, let me think... something like three dots. I can't remember if it was the left or the right side...hmmmm." The Professor disappeared into thought again as he tried to remember.

"Not critical, Professor. You've been most helpful; most helpful indeed. If we catch up with Popfarmel, we may need to call on you again. In the meantime, our technical staff will be in touch to design that detector."

Lort returned once again to the call from somewhere deep in one of his brains. "Oh, yes, yes, any time, any time at all. The detector; yes, yes. I'll watch for your holo-call." And with that, he returned to his thoughts as he signed off the call.

Lentipede was ecstatic. "Fantastic! That must be how Farpel is appearing in multiple places; holo-projections through micro-rifts! And those kiosks at the mall; popping up through a rift, and disappearing the same way!"

"On top of everything else, I'm pretty certain that Popfarmel and Farpelmop are one and the same. Bring up that hologram of Farplemop, will you, Mop?"

The three of them proceeded to observe a hologram of Farpelmop slowly rotating in front of them. After a moment, Sharboff was the first to point at the projection. "Look at that! On Farpelmop's left side; those three marks!"

Lentipede practically jumped out of his net. "Well, that does it for me. Popfarmel and Farpelmop are the same Kinglorf."

"All right, you two heard what the Professor had to say. Get down to the Technical Department, get back in touch with Professor Lort, and let's get that detector built!"

Sharboff jumped in, so to speak. "But Chief Inspector, Farpelmop could create a rift virtually anywhere; how do we know where to place the detector? You heard the professor; searching generally in our dimensional space will be like trying to find a black hole in a dark void!"

"Don't you see, Sharboff? We know Farpel is moving these kiosks in and out of malls through dimensional rifts, particularly on Kor. All we have to do is place our detectors at the malls, and wait. We'll get a signal as soon as a kiosk pops up, and we can at least grab one of Farpel's associates in the act! Go, go, get to work on that detector."

Mop and Sharboff were making their way down to the Technical Department, when Mop looked at her with two of his four eyes, and spoke up. "Well, Sharboff, what do you think are the odds that this is going to be successful?"

Sharboff returned the look. "I have a feeling this is going to be a total waste of time, to tell you the truth. We're going to need an awful lot of detectors to cover all the malls, even if we restrict ourselves to Kor. And even then, suppose we get a signal? By the time we get there, the kiosk will probably be gone. But I guess we'd better humor the Chief Inspector until something better comes along."

11.250^{12}

"Have we had any reports on those detectors we disseminated at the malls on Kor?" It had been almost a Towlak month since detectors had been placed at the malls, in an effort to identify the energy fluctuations attributable to Farpelmop's interdimensional shenanigans. Pop-up kiosks selling druzhia continued to come and go, and Chief Inspector Lentipede's patience was at the breaking point.

Mop and Sharboff were in the meeting with Lentipede, and Mop spoke up. "Well, Chief Inspector, as you know, we've experienced 32 separate identifiable energy fluctuations with the detectors. Of those, 11 events were attributable to kids playing with cheap energy-leaking particle colliders in the mall while their parents were shopping, and we think another one was caused by a faulty GadgiYack that somebody left on a table in front of our detector. Based on interviews at the scene, we think the remaining 20 were definitely the result of energy fluctuations due to interdimensional openings, but by the time any of our agents arrived, we couldn't find anything unusual."

Lentipede looked discouraged, waving his tentacles slowly back and forth (which is, after all, how a Towlak appears discouraged). "Well, I said those detectors would be a complete waste of time, but does anybody ever listen to me? No; of course not!"

Sharboff opened her orifice to say something on the subject, but a look from three of Mop's four eyes told her that discretion was the order of the day. They sat contemplating the issue briefly.

An annoying signal started beeping on a panel, but Lentipede was too wrapped up in thought to hear it. After a short interval, Mop transitioned to the panel and observed some text in the air. He then proceeded to interrupt Lentipede's thought process. "Chief Inspector, we're getting a holo-call from someone on Measel who would like to speak with us about that Farpelmop hologram we disseminated throughout the Trading League."

Lentipede bolted upright in his net. "Of course! Bring up their projection!" A holo-call opened before the group, showing a Measeloot. A Measeloot with markedly large appendages.

"Hello, hello, are you there?" Kolameas Elwinkem appeared before them, and thanks to modern Holo-CalloMatic technology, her name was projected directly above her.

Lentipede took the lead. "Yes, we're here. How may we help you? I understand you're calling regarding a hologram we recently distributed on your planet."

Kolameas jumped up and down with excitement. "Yes, yes, I've seen him, this Farlemop fellow! I've seen him here on Measel!"

"Um, yes, it's actually Farpelmop. Please continue; when did you see him last? And what were the circumstances at the time you saw him?"

"Well, I can't remember exactly when; it was, like, a few months ago here on Measel, I think. Yes, it was definitely a few months. I saw him at a restaurant. Oh dear, I can't remember the name, but I know it's owned by Willodig Propmeasel, because Willodig is the cousin of Brobding, whose mother Measella Wishkonky is a friend of my mother, and she, Measella, that is, introduced me to Brobding, who's a friend of *mine*, well, he's not really what I'd call a *friend* at this point, since it seems to me that he keeps trying to avoid me *all* the time, but he's still interested in me, well, at least I *think* he's still interested in me. Do you think he's still interested in me? Oh dear, what was the question again?"

Lentipede prepared himself for a very long and potentially unhelpful conversation.

"Ms….Elwinkem, is it? Why don't we slow down a bit and take the questions one at a time. First, what were the particular circumstances that brought about your sighting of Farpelmop?"

Kolameas Elwinkem had been mumbling to herself on some topic or other as Chief Inspector Lentipede tried to remain in control of the conversation. She paused as she detected a question from the Chief Inspector.

"Circumstances? What, oh, you mean why did I see that guy Farmelop? Well, Willodig, you know, that's Brobding's cousin; did I mention that his mother, that's Brobding's mother, is a friend of my mother? Anyway, what was I saying? Oh yes, Willodig clued me in that Brobding would be at his restaurant that night, so I went over to see him, Brobding, that is, and there they were!"

Lentipede tried his best to remain calm. In the background, Mop and Sharboff were in the process of giggling, or the equivalent thereof for their respective species. "Please, Ms. Elwinkem, let's try to concentrate. Can you name all the parties you saw at the restaurant when you arrived?"

Kolameas managed to stay focused, in a manner of speaking, for the moment. "Oh, there weren't any parties; no, no, the restaurant wasn't even open! No, the only ones there were myself, Brobding, and that guy Larfepom."

Lentipede decided it was pointless to keep correcting the name. "And what were Brobding and Farmelpop doing when you arrived, Ms.

Elwinkem?" Lentipede froze for a moment as he finished the sentence, and thought to himself, 'Now she has *me* doing it! It's Farpelmop! Farpelmop!' He looked sternly at Mop and Sharboff just as they were about to break into serious laughter; the smiles disappeared for the moment.

Kolameas thought briefly. "Well, they were just sort of talking, and Brobding told me they had some important business, or something like that; yes, it was definitely important business. And then he rushed me out the door! Can you believe it? Right out the door! I'll tell you, if I didn't know better, I would think Brobding is trying to send me a message or something. Goodness!"

Lentipede didn't think he could get much additional useful information from Kolameas Elwinkem, except for one important last question. "Tell me, Ms. Elwinkem, can you give us some contact information for this Brobding...?"

"Measelfort, his name is Brobding Measelfort. I'll send you the holo-call number I have for him; mind you, not that he ever answers when

I call! And I know he works for the MITE Corporation, fixing this and that in those transdermal thingywidget tubes of theirs."

Lentipede and his team finally had a new lead to pursue. "Thank you, Ms. Elwinkem, you've been most helpful. If we may, we'll get back to you if we have any further questions."

Kolameas smiled. "Of course, of course! At least *somebody* will call me back! Honestly, I just don't know what to make of that Brobding and his..." The words trailed off as Kolameas moved away from her Holo-CalloMatic, leaving it in the 'on' position in the process. Mop disconnected the call from their end.

Lentipede was pleased, and ready for some action. "All right, we have work to do. Mop, see if you can track down Brobding Measelfort, and let's have a conversation with him as soon as possible. He may be not only a lead, but a suspect! While you're at it, check the MITE Corporation database; it may have some useful information on him. And Sharboff, at the same time, let's see about some surveillance on this Measelfort; maybe he can lead us somewhere interesting."

12.292[13]

Brobding Measelfort was, as always, diligently at work in a transdimensional transport tube; this particular day, he was working proximate to the planet Sleebort 5. If not properly attired for the occasion (about which the MITE Corporation has reminded them again and again), Sleebortikans (which is how one refers to those from Sleebort 5) had a nasty habit of depositing a slimy and rather persistent residue on the transport tube surfaces as they moved from one planet to another. As distasteful as it was to contend with this slime, it was part of Brobding's job to remove it. It was a relatively simple task for him to spray on a special solvent; this would cause the residue to turn into an easily managed powdery substance.

In the method sanctioned by both the Trading League and the MITE Corporation for removing the powder, Brobding would install a remotely controlled portal on the wall of the tube, behind which he had created a carefully controlled micro-rift in the tube wall.

At that point, making sure that no one was transiting through the transport tube in question, Brobding would: close the atmospheric containment doors at the nearest two ends of the tube; remotely open the portal that he established earlier; evacuate the powder into the most convenient, and ideally vacant, dimensional space; and reclose the portal. He would then effect a repair on the micro-rift, and reopen the atmospheric containment doors to traffic.

As another approach, of course, he could simply take out a small vacuum cleaner and suck up the powder.

He was engaged in the latter approach when his Holo-CalloMatic projected the following message:

PLANetary SECURITY TEam AND REconnaissANCE DIVISION
PLANET TOWL

DO YOU WISH TO ACCEPT THE HOLO-CALL? IF NOT, PLEASE SELECT:
1. IGNORE THEM; THEY'RE ANNOYING ANYWAY
2. REJECT THEM IN A NASTY FASHION BECAUSE THEY'RE SO ANNOYING
3. REJECT THEM, BUT TRY TO SEEM A BIT GUILTY FOR DOING SO
4. REJECT THEM IN A FRIENDLY WAY; MAYBE THEY'LL CALL BACK LATER

Brobding found these new emotion-enabled Holo-CalloMatics somewhat irritating, but as he was a Measeloot, and quite congenial by nature, he didn't complain to anyone about it. He looked at the identification on the call, and thought to himself 'Now why would PLASTERED be calling me? Some sort of illicit activity in the transdimensional transport tubes, perhaps?' He accepted the call, and a Chienolian appeared before him. For reasons unknown, it seemed to be wearing a strikingly fluffy pink fur coat.

"Brobding Measelfort? This is Kerolirolia Sharboff from the PLAnetary Security TEam and REconnaissance Division. Do you have a moment? We have a few questions." And that's exactly how Sharboff pronounced the name of the organization, with serious accents on the 'PLA,' 'S,' 'TE,' etc.

Brobding knew a few Chienolians; most of them seemed reasonably friendly. "Well, I'm in the process of cleaning up some Sleebortikan slime powder, but I think I can manage a few moments. How may I help you?"

Of a sudden, two other figures appeared before him. "I'm Chief Inspector Lentipede, and this is my associate Mop. You've already been introduced to Sharboff. Mr. Measelfort, we'd like to ask you about your association with one Dearlotin Farpelmop, also known as Loteardin Popfarmel."

Brobding thought for a moment; he couldn't think of anyone with those names, but the name did seem familiar. "I'm sorry, Chief Inspector, but I don't recall knowing anyone by those particular names."

Sharboff thought of something. "Perhaps there's a chance you might know him as 'Farpel.'"

Brobding froze, and turned an interesting shade of green. As an aside, and for reasons that should now be obvious, Measeloots are not renowned for their prowess at the poker table. He tried to turn back to his more customary orange hue, without success. For Measeloots, honesty really was the only policy. "Oh, yes! I met Farpel at my cousin Willodig's restaurant on Measel. What would you like to know, Chief Inspector?"

Lentipede knew he had this Measeloot cornered now; if he wasn't sure earlier, the green coloring confirmed it for him. "Well, Mr. Measelfort, we understand from a reliable source that you have had some business dealings with Mr. Farpel. Can you tell us the nature of the business?" On hearing the expression 'reliable source,' Mop and Sharboff started giggling again as they recalled the conversation with Kolameas Elwinkem.

Brobding gathered his thoughts before replying, and also took a moment to consider who might have spilled the proverbial zoopels (that would be 'beans' for those of the Earthly persuasion). "Well, Chief Inspector, Farpel and

I had discussed distributing some tea to planets in the Trading League, but I haven't seen him for some months now." Unfortunately, the interesting shade of green became even more pronounced as Brobding spoke, and he seemed to be speaking in a rather shrill voice that he was unable to tone down.

Lentipede was confused. "Tea, Mr. Measelfort? I'm not acquainted with that material. Perhaps you can clarify what that is for us."

"Oh, yes, I believe it's referred to as 'druzhia' in the Trading League." Brobding observed a noticeable reaction from the PLASTERED team, and was not happy that he had let that one slip by. In the meantime, the shrillness wouldn't budge.

"And tell us, Mr. Measelfort, why would Farpel be interested in discussing such business with you?"

Brobding didn't want to get Mrs. Hensworthy in any trouble; he thought fast. "Well, I'm sure it's because of my expert knowledge of the transdimensional transport tubes." The green was positively electric at this point.

Lentipede knew something was up. "Thank you, Mr. Measelfort. We appreciate your cooperation. You wouldn't happen to know where we might find Farpel at present?"

"No, as I mentioned, I haven't seen him for some time now." At this point, Brobding just wanted the call to end.

"Well, thank you again, Mr. Measelfort. We'll be in touch if we have any further questions." And with waves on both sides, Lentipede disconnected. He was excited.

"We have him on the run now. Sharboff, I'm now convinced that some surveillance on this guy is our best bet. Did you get some orbitons planted near him, so we can keep a set of eyes on him?"

"Just placed, Chief Inspector. We needed to determine his locations first; as a high level tech for the MITE Corporation, he's all over the transdimensional transport tubes, so we've had to place quite a few orbitons in order to ensure continuous coverage. Nothing exciting to report so far; just repair activities in the tubes."

"Also, we encountered a little delay. The Technical Department only had the old ON-64633 orbitons, which hadn't been used in a while. They were kind of dusty, and, as I'm sure you know, they're pretty conspicuous, especially with those long visi-stalks that hold the holographic capture technology. I had to wait for Tech to get some of the newer ON-76776 models, which are much flatter."

"Yes, yes, don't bother me with the technical details. Sharboff. Hopefully this call we had with Measelfort will change the picture, so to speak, and he'll make the mistake we've been waiting for. Mop, any interesting data on the guy?"

"Well, Chief Inspector, from what I've found, he's pretty much a model employee of the MITE Corporation; no prior illicit activities, and he gets the job done."

Lentipede was practically vibrating. "All right, gang, it's up to the surveillance now. Let's see what we can find out."

13.750[14]

It was a customarily chilly autumn afternoon in Hampsthwaite as Mrs. Hensworthy enjoyed her tea before a comforting fire. Malthorp was out and about; they had finished the bottle of their favorite pre-prandial sherry, and Malthorp had gone out in search of a replacement.

Unfortunately, he had rather overindulged in the beverage as he and Mrs. Hensworthy considered their dinner plans the previous evening. As I'm sure you recall, Malthorp is a Jordalakian, and Jordalakian physiology tends to react rather oddly when exposed to excess quantities of alcohol. Malthorp had forgotten about this as he sat before the fire, thoroughly enjoying the beverage. Mrs. Hensworthy was in the kitchen at the time, considering the options with respect to the evening's cuisine.

As Malthorp sipped his third glass of delicious sherry, he proceeded to revert in a fairly uncontrollable fashion to his former gelatinous self, except for one eye and an oral orifice, and a portion of his form cascaded down the front of the chair on which he resided. The orifice spoke.

"Eleanora, my dear, I am having a bit of an issue. Please don't be alarmed at the prospect, but unfortunately, I seem to have revisited my Jordalakian form. A bit much on the sherry side, I'm afraid. I'll be able to return to my Malthorpian configuration as soon as I process this beverage. I would suggest, however, that we not invite any neighbors for the moment."

Mrs. Hensworthy returned to the living room from the kitchen, and observed the blob that now constituted Malthorp as it resided on the chair, down the chair front, and nominally, on the rug before the fire.

"Oh dear, Malthorp, you are looking rather, well, gelatinous at the moment. How long shall it be before you can pull yourself together, so to speak, and revert to your handsome self?"

Malthorp considered the issue. "Well, I'd suggest a fairly late dinner this evening, my dear. I should say two to three Earth hours, and I'll be able to regain my, shall we say, composure."

And sure enough, two hours and 27 minutes later, Malthorp had returned to human form, except for somewhat droopy ears that dropped over each side of the chair, and which corrected themselves approximately 17 minutes and 12 seconds later. But back to our story.

As Mrs. Hensworthy enjoyed her tea the following day, she heard the customary 'whooshing' sound of an interdimensional rift as it formed within the opening of her bookcase. Moments later, Brobding Measelfort stepped through into her living room, and began to speak in quite an animated fashion.

Unfortunately, Mrs. Hensworthy heard only a collection of squeaks and clicks, and held up her hand, indicating that Brobding should pause momentarily. She then reached into a handy drawer in the side table adjacent to her chair, withdrew her GadgiYack, and placed it in a convenient nostril. Her left nostril, actually.

"Ah, that's better. Now, Mr. Measelfort, how lovely to see you! It has been too long. And how is that nice Mr. Farpel? He's been leaving the most delightful diamonds here in the living room now and then as payment for the tea we've been providing. Our local jeweler friend has told us that they're of the most extraordinary quality! With the excellent proceeds, Malthorp and I are actually thinking about buying a small vacation cottage in the Port Isaac area. We do so enjoy our Cornwall vacations."

Brobding was practically vibrating with anticipation, and finally managed to get a word in. "Hello, Mrs. Hensworthy; it is so nice to see you as well. If you please, I would like to speak with you on a subject of some importance!"

"Oh, I beg your pardon, Mr. Measelfort, but I do tend to go on. Please tell me what might be on your mind, or minds, as the case may be."

Brobding could barely get the words out. "Well, Mrs. Hensworthy, I had a call from a Chief Inspector Lentipede from PLASTERED, and he was asking about Farpel and the tea!"

Mrs. Hensworthy wore a somewhat confused expression. "'Plastered,' Mr. Measelfort? I'm afraid I'm not acquainted with that organization."

"Oh, yes, I should have realized. It's the PLAnetary Security TEam and REconnaissance Division, the constabulary force that has overall policing responsibility within the Trading League."

Mrs. Hensworthy's expression turned to one of concern. "Oh dear; when Mr. Farpel undertook the tea distribution on our behalf, I believe I understood him to say he would keep this sort of thing under control. And we don't want to be getting you into any trouble, Mr. Measelfort. Why do you think they called you, rather than call that nice Mr. Farpel directly?"

"From what they asked on the call, I don't think they know where he is. He hasn't visited recently, by any chance?"

"Why, no, we haven't seen Mr. Farpel for quite some time now. He simply retrieves the tea shipment from our supplier, and leaves the occasional little bag of diamonds here in the living room. He must be delivering the diamonds at very odd hours, as neither Malthorp nor I have observed him dropping them off."

Now Brobding looked concerned. "Well, I certainly don't know where he is at this point, and I think it's important that we let him know about Chief Inspector Lentipede. Perhaps my cousin Willodig can help me get in touch with him again. After all, it was Willodig who connected me to Farpel in the first place. If you see him, please inform him about the inquiries from PLASTERED. We may need to consider going out of business soon."

"Oh, dear, that would be unfortunate, but we don't want trouble with the law. I'll certainly watch for Mr. Farpel, and catch him up if I should see him. In the meantime, I hope that cousin of yours can help."

Brobding bid adieu to Mrs. Hensworthy, stepped back through the rift, and sealed the opening. The passage to the kitchen appeared once again, as if the rift had never existed.

As this was transpiring, and just a short while later by almost any planetary standard, interesting things were happening on another planet, in a different dimensional 3-space; specifically, on the planet Towl. Mop had just hurried into Chief Inspector Lentipede's office.

Before we continue, we wish to clarify the statement 'short while later,' in deference to the inhabitants of the planet Whicket 2. Using Earth measurements, as those are the ones with which the reader may be most likely acquainted, Whicket 2 rotates 360 degrees about its axis in approximately 12 Earth minutes, and revolves around its star in 2.4 Earth days. It isn't a terribly productive planet, as the inhabitants spend most of their time attending birthday parties. On Whicket 2, a 'short while later' would be a very short while indeed, from the Earthling's perspective. But let's get back to our story.

"Chief Inspector! One of our orbitons has just captured some activity that you need to see!" Mop's tentacles were twitching in excitement. He entered the Chief Inspector's office and touched a panel; a hologram appeared before them.

Lentipede peered at it closely. "Wait a minute...is that...is that Measelport I'm seeing here? What is he up to?"

Mop pointed at a portion of the projection. "Uh, excuse me, Chief Inspector, but I believe it's Measel*fort*. Please watch what happens right here at time point 2:27:15." They both observed intently as Brobding opened a noticeable rift in the transdimensional transport tube wall. Lentipede practically fell back in his net.

"Well I'll be a gridnap's progeny!! Did he just open an interdimensional portal in the side of that transdimensional tube?! Where is that, exactly? And just as importantly, where does that portal lead to?!"

Mop checked on the location of the orbiton in question. "That would be orbiton 3a75xt, which is in...." He hesitated as he examined a list projected in front of him. "...ah, it appears to be a transdimensional transport tube accessing the Grange planets in 3-space 784.

I'm sorry, Chief Inspector, but I'm not sure what's adjacent to that transdimensional tube, or what 3-space might define the adjacent regions."

Lentipede was turning deeper shades of orange as he contemplated the implications. "Does that Measelfort have any idea what he's doing?! He could introduce incompatible alien species to the Trading League n-space, or cause crazy interdimensional changes! Where's Sharboff? Sharboff!"

A moment later, Kerolirolia Sharboff ambled in. "You bellowed, Chief Inspector?"

"Yes, Sharboff, you're a Chienolian, so this job's for you. Get that guy Lorkin Lort on a holo-call, you know, the Professor at the Center for Education in the Galactic Sciences on Lechien 7. We need some answers about the n-space in the vicinity of the Grange planets, and we need the answers fast."

Lorkin Lort briefly abandoned a lecture he was delivering to a group of Interdimensional Physics grad students on n-space repercussions derived from perturbations in a wholly enveloped 3-space; his assistant had informed him of a holo-call that claimed to be urgent. "This is Professor Lorkin Lort, how may I...oh, Chief Inspector! And your associates, how nice to see you all again!"

Lentipede was feeling quite anxious. "Sorry to drag you away from your work, Professor, but we have an issue here, and need your valuable insight."

Lorkin nodded. "Not at all, Chief Inspector; I'm always pleased to help our friends at PLASTERED. Tell me, what's on your mind or minds?"

Lentipede jumped right in. "We've been tracking a Measeloot by the name of Brobding Measelfort, Professor. He's a highly skilled technician of the MITE Corporation, and we just observed him opening an intentional interdimensional portal in the wall of a transdimensional transport tube. Our side of the opening is in a tube accessing the Grange planets; we have no clue where the other side is. We were hoping you might have some ideas."

Lorkin Lort thought for a moment; that name sounded really familiar. "Did you say 'Measelfort'? You know, I've come across that name before. Give me a moment...yes, I remember now! He was that very nice Measeloot who had been sent to repair a rift created by that group... what were they called again? Oh yes, the Planetarials, an isolationist group that wanted to shut down the transdimensional transport tubes, because they didn't want off-planet competition for their particular brand of foot fungus powder, or something along those lines. I seem to recall that Measelfort unfortunately fell through the rift into Barnork 3-space. Luckily, he ended up in the living room of that very nice human, Mrs. Hensworthy. She did serve a particularly lovely beverage; I believe she referred to it as tea."

Lentipede, Mop and Sharboff fell out of their nets at the mention of tea.

"Did you say '*tea*,' Professor?! What else can you tell us about Measelfort and this Mrs. Hensworthy? And most importantly, is there any danger in having this portal open into the Barnork system?"

Lorkin shook his tentacles. "To answer your last question first, Chief Inspector, I don't think it's particularly dangerous to be open to Mrs. Hensworthy's living room, unless members of her species start to transition into our dimensional spaces. From what I recall, Mrs. Hensworthy seemed to be a congenial and fairly discreet creature. I wouldn't leave the breach in place for too long, however."

"As for Measelfort and Mrs. Hensworthy themselves, there's not much more to say from my perspective. I examined the opening with my team, we all enjoyed a nice round of tea and tasty morsels, and then that fellow Measelfort proceeded to close the rift."

Lentipede was thrilled. "Thank you, Professor; you've been most helpful once again."

"My pleasure, Chief Inspector; call on me anytime. Now I really should return to that lecture." And with that, Lorkin disconnected.

"That's it! That's got to be it! Measelfort made some kind of deal with Farpelmop, and is sourcing the tea from outside the Trading League through an interdimensional rift! But how are they moving the stuff to the forbidden planets? They can't be bringing it all through that rift made my Measelfort!"

Sharboff chimed in. "Well, Chief Inspector, couldn't Farpelmop be creating channels for the goods using interdimensional folding in an alternative n-space? I mean, he did it for pop-up kiosks in our space, why not extend it into the Barnork 3-space?"

"Sharboff, you're brilliant!" Sharboff was all smiles as Lentipede continued. "That must be the way Farpelmop is moving the stuff from place to place. He wouldn't need the transdimensional tubes at all!"

"Since we can't seem to catch Farpelmop in the act, we'll need to get to this Hensworthy creature, and cut off Farpelmop's supply line. And the easiest way to do that is through Measelfort. Bring him in."

15.000[15]

Brobding Measelfort was one unhappy Measeloot. He had been unable to connect with Dearlotin Farpelmop; even his favorite cousin Willodig didn't know where Farpelmop was hiding. And when Farpelmop wanted to hide, no one was going to find him. With his ability to operate in n dimensions, they wouldn't even know where to start looking.

Brobding had been working on a tricky transdimensional transport tube repair when two agents from PLASTERED approached him and had him accompany them to PLASTERED Headquarters on Towl. Getting to Towl from his previous location had required a tedious journey through three separate transdimensional tubes, and Brobding was tired. At least the agents allowed him to complete the repair before they took him away.

Now he was waiting in an interrogation room at the offices of Chief Inspector Lentipede. He had no idea what was going to happen to him, but he had already decided that the tea trade simply wasn't worth the legal challenges. However, he wasn't sure that he could convince Farpelmop of that. And he certainly didn't want to end up eating vegetables on the Whoola planets.

Brobding could already hear his overbearing Aunt, Measelanna Hooscod, lecturing him for straying from his steady job at the MITE Corporation. She was always looking for an excuse to be annoying.

As he was mulling this over, a door opened, and in walked two Towlaks and a Chienolian. He had forgotten how ugly Towlaks were in a face-to-face situation. Of course, Towlaks thought the same thing about Measeloots, but luckily, everyone just tried to get along.

"Mr. Measelfort? I am Chief Inspector Lentipede. These are my associates, Mop and Sharboff. I believe you met them earlier on our holo-call."

Tentacles were waved all around in recognition of the attendees.

"Let's talk about Dearlotin Farpelmop, also known as Farpel. We want to know where he is, and what he's up to. In particular, where is he getting the druzhia that's being dropped on four forbidden planets in the Trading League, and how is he shipping the stuff?"

Brobding vibrated nervously, and once again turned a curious shade of green. "I don't know! I don't know where he is! I don't know anything! All I wanted was to do something more interesting than transdimensional tube repair, and look where it's gotten me!"

"Now, now, it won't help to get excited, Mr. Measelfort. We know you had a meeting with him, so you have some involvement in this."

"And we know a lot more. For example, we know you created an interdimensional rift in a transdimensional transport tube in order to meet with a Mrs. Hensworthy of Barnork 3."

Brobding's color approximated British Racing Green by this time. How could they possibly know about Mrs. Hensworthy? He knew it was no use lying; he'd just turn more and more iridescent shades of green every time he tried to deceive them. "All right! I'll tell you! Mrs. Hensworthy makes a wonderful cup of tea, and I was hoping we might be able to introduce the tea into the Trading League! Honestly, I didn't know anything about druzhia or forbidden planets! Mrs. Hensworthy developed a source of supply, and Farpel moves the stuff. That's all I know! And you should leave Mrs. Hensworthy alone! She hasn't done anything wrong! There! I told you, and I'm glad!" By this time, the room was in sympathetic vibration with Brobding due to the intensity with which he was shaking.

"Now, now, Mr. Measelfort; we certainly appreciate your candor, but either this supply to the forbidden planets needs to be squashed, or we need to figure out another way to resolve this. After all, the substance *is* banned on those planets." Suddenly, an interesting thought occurred to the Chief Inspector, but he chose to keep it to himself for the time being.

Brobding nodded dejectedly. "I don't know how we can stop him now; Farpel, that is. He's operating around all of us at this point. He picks up the tea, and he delivers the tea, and we never see him! And he's not even using the transport tubes; he operates in an alternative n-space! He's unstoppable, I tell you."

The group sat for some time, considering what they had just heard from Brobding Measelfort. Lentipede knew what he had to do. "I don't think we need to detain you any further, Mr. Measelfort. You are free to go; after all, we have bigger Kinglorfs to catch."

Brobding faded noticeably, back to a fairly light green tone, and wasn't sure what to say. "Thank you! I really... I don't... Thank you!" He then hurriedly left the facility.

Back in his office with Mop and Sharboff, Lentipede sat back in his net. "I think I have a surefire way of stopping Farpelmop's druzhia trade." It was clear from his demeanor that the Chief Inspector was fairly obsessed with Farpelmop as a worthy opponent. "I think we need to bring in another party, someone who will make an offer to Farpelmop that he can't refuse." Mop and Sharboff weren't sure what he had in mind, but, looking at him, they were a little concerned regarding the Chief Inspector's sanity.

A reasonable number of Earthly rotations occurred before Brobding Measelfort heard anything more about tea. As far as he was concerned, he would have been more than happy to never hear about it again, but there was no escaping his involvement now.

He received a recorded Holo-call from Farpel, informing him of an imminent meeting at the Hensworthy residence. Farpel made it clear that absence was not an option. Brobding started vibrating again, and did his best not to turn green. He really didn't enjoy these excitations.

The appointed hour arrived, and Brobding made his way to the appropriate point in the transdimensional transport tube. He set his tools down, looked around carefully, and suddenly realized how Chief Inspector Lentipede had known about the rift. There, on a far wall of the tube, was a miniscule orbiton!

Brobding drew from his tool kit a small blob of transdimensional concrete, used to repair wall damage in the transport tubes. He then carefully sidled up to the orbiton, as inconspicuously as possible, and quickly placed the blob onto the lens of the device. "That ought to keep them out of my fur for a while." Brobding hummed in a manner that other Measeloots might interpret as a chuckle, and, returning to the proper location on the tube wall, once again opened a precisely sized rift in the midst of Mrs. Hensworthy's bookcase.

Mrs. Hensworthy was sitting in her customary chair by the fireplace, with Malthorp in the chair across from her. He had been careful with the sherry since his recent rather gelatinous incident, and so he was in full Malthorpian form.

They both turned to observe Brobding stepping through the rift, and moments later, Dearlotin Farpelmop dropped through a rift in the ceiling and floated to the floor.

Mrs. Hensworthy was the first to speak. "Well, I see we're all gathered for Mr. Farpel's meeting. I must say, Mr. Farpel, I was rather surprised to find a holographic projection speaking to me from the butter container inside my refrigerator! That was a most curious manner of invitation."

Farpel settled himself on the floor. "Yea, my aim was a little off on that one."

Mrs. Hensworthy continued. "No harm done, Mr. Farpel. May I offer everyone a round of tea?"

Brobding winced noticeably at the mention of tea; tinges of green appeared around his extremities. "Please, Mrs. Hensworthy, the very mention of the word 'tea' is causing me to change color."

Farpel chimed in. "We need to get down to business anyway, creatures. I just found out from various contacts, who shall remain nameless, that a character named Lentipede, a bigwig at PLASTERED, has some curious connections with the druzhia monopoly operating in the Trading League. I think he might even be a crooked Towlak, but I'm not one to hold *that* against him. What I *do* hold against him is that he's convinced the druzhia gang to pay off key politicians on the four forbidden planets in order to have druzhia legalized there, and undoubtedly make his job easier. It's also pretty clear that Lentipede told his druzhia buddies about our tea operation, because I received a nasty message from them telling us to back off. They said it's their turf now." The group sat in silence for few moments, and then Farpel continued.

"Well, Meas, I told you what the druzhia cartel does to those who step on their tea leaves, so to speak. Mrs. Hensworthy, I think we'll need to have a going-out-of-business sale, before the cartel starts to get nasty. As for that annoying guy Lentipede, I have an interesting idea where we might dump any leftovers."

After that conversation, Mrs. Hensworthy fairly insisted that they enjoy a nice soothing cup of tea before they adjourn. She then turned to Brobding. "Don't fret about it, Mr. Measelfort; it was fun while it lasted, but perhaps we can find some other product of interest for you to offer to the Trading League."

Both Farpel and Brobding considered Mrs. Hensworthy's comment, and Farpel responded, "Well, Meas, give it some thought. If you come up with an idea, and you want to get together on the distribution, you can find me through that cousin of yours. In the meantime, I have one or two loose ends to close up, and then I think I'll lay low for a while. I don't need that Lentipede giving me a hard time."

"Hensworthys, it's been an interesting experience. I may drop in from time to time. Meas is right; you do make a good cup of tea. Later!" And with that, Farpel rose to the ceiling, and drifted through the interdimensional rift he had created there. The rift closed up behind him, and the ceiling returned to its unassuming self, with that nice dentil crown molding around the edges.

Within a couple of Earth weeks, all (or at least most) had returned to normal. Brobding Measelfort was working diligently, making various intricate repairs to keep the transdimensional transport tubes fully operational. At the same time, he was thinking about what Earthly products might be of interest within the Trading League. Meanwhile, Mrs. Hensworthy had made arrangements with the tea distributors to bring to a close their deliveries of tea to the shipping container on the distributor's property. As I'm sure you recall, Farpel had retrieved the tea periodically by creating an interdimensional rift that opened directly into the container.

Some Earth days later, Chief Inspector Lentipede came to his office as usual, opened the door, and was confronted of a sudden with an impenetrable wall of tea leaves. His entire office had been completely packed, like a solid brick, with tea. It was said that, even without an interdimensional rift, beings in alternate 3-spaces could hear Lentipede crying out, "Farpellllllll!!"

When he regained some form of composure, he proceeded to bellow for assistance. "Mop! Sharboff! Call the maintenance staff!! We have a problem here! And tell them to start boiling water; I hope everyone in the agency likes druzhia!"

As for Dearlotin Farpelmop, he was last seen vacationing on Wowserlik 3, the renowned beach planet. Interestingly enough, he was seen in the company of Kolameas Elwinkem. He never could resist those big appendages.

<<<<>>>>

Stay tuned for the next exciting adventure!...

B

www.ingramcontent.com/pod-product-compliance
Lightning Source LLC
Chambersburg PA
CBHW071303130626
46556CB00003B/1451